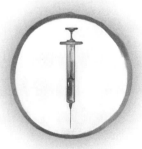

King
Needle

Kingdom of Needle and Bone

MIRA GRANT

Subterranean Press 2018

First Edition

ISBN
978-1-59606-871-1

Subterranean Press
PO Box 190106
Burton, MI 48519

subterraneanpress.com

Manufactured in the United States of America

For Kathleen Sloan

"...people want to make this about politics: want to pretend there aren't consequences for choosing not to immunize a child. After all, if everyone else immunizes, their children won't get sick, right? The vaccine will protect the immunized children, and the unimmunized will remain pure, untouched by the filthy manmade miracle of modern medicine. Their bodies will be lowered into their graves devoid of the imaginary poisons that have replaced smallpox and polio and measles as the bogeymen haunting a parent's heart.

That isn't how herd immunity works. That isn't how vaccination works. That isn't how being part of a compassionate society works. Even setting aside the risk to the children whose parents choose to not to vaccinate—and as a medical professional, uttering the phrase 'setting aside the risk to children' breaks my heart—even taking that terrible, monstrous step does not protect our most vulnerable populations from a violent crime disguised as a personal choice. How dare you. How *dare* you."

—excerpt from op-ed by Dr. Isabelle Gauley,
The Concord Times.

PART I: Ring Around the Rosies

1: | Patient Zero

1.

LISA MORRIS had been vaccinated according to her pediatrician's recommended schedule, receiving her first dose of synthesized protection from the dangers of the world when she was two months old. Her parents had asked questions about each shot. They were scientifically-minded people who listened to their doctor, believing that years of medical school held more value than afternoons on Wikipedia, and they had approved the injections, one after the other, allowing their beloved daughter to build the most robust immune system possible.

Lisa had never been a fan of getting shots—what child was? What adult was, for that matter? An injection is an injection, no matter how great the potential rewards—but she had always enjoyed the ice cream that followed, and once she was old enough, she had learned to enjoy the subtle untensing of her parents' shoulders. She was still young, eight years old, and sheltered enough not to understand everything that was happening in the world around her. She knew that some of the kids she went to school with didn't get their shots, because of what they called a "personal exemption," which was supposed to be about believing in God and thinking He would make everything better, even when that wasn't true.

"If you don't want them poking you with a needle anymore, all you have to say is you believe in Jesus and that makes it a sin," one of the girls in Lisa's class had said, smugly superior in her ability to beat the system.

Lisa, who understood Jesus the same way she understood Santa Claus—as a distant, powerful, potentially fictional figure who nonetheless had good things to teach about generosity and honesty and compassion—had frowned, and asked, "Would Jesus want me to lie?"

"Pretty sure Jesus doesn't want us getting poked with needles," the girl had replied.

Lisa had gone home, and thought a lot about Jesus and what He might want, and had come to the conclusion that if He existed, He wouldn't want her to use Him to tell lies to her parents. She had not claimed religion. She had received her flu shot, the same way she always did, and when the girl in her class missed two whole weeks of school and had to stay into the summer to make up the time, Lisa had done her best not to be smug about it. Lying to Jesus did not, it seemed, pay.

That had been months ago, at the start of vacation. Now September was looming, and with it would come another year of math problems and essays and people standing outside her aunt's practice with signs, chanting about how they had the right to make their own choices about their own children. It was sort of funny how some parents acted like kids couldn't make up their own minds or make their own decisions, but could still get in trouble for doing stuff. Lisa sort of thought it was wrong, for parents to act like they were and weren't people at the same time, and all because they were young.

Mostly, though, Lisa thought she didn't feel good. Her mouth was dry and her nose was running and her head was spinning and her skin felt like it was two sizes too small, like she was going to burst out of it if she moved too quickly. She scowled at her reflection in the bathroom mirror of the hotel room she was sharing with her parents. They were probably going to say she'd spent too much time in the sun and if she was going to be sick, they'd be better off staying at the hotel and letting her rest, rather than turning it into sunstroke. And maybe they'd be right, but this was the *end* of the summer, and they were flying home from Florida *tomorrow.* If she wanted to ride the big coasters one more time, it had to be today.

Had she been older than eight, she might have understood that the kind of unwell she was feeling wasn't normal, wasn't sunstroke, wasn't something she should hide. Had she been younger than eight, she might have gone whining to her mother before she realized that she ran the risk of cancelling the day's adventure. Had she been any other age, she would still have died, but she might not have taken quite so many people with her.

2.

AFTER THE outbreak, people hypothesized that the new strain of measles—dubbed "Morris's disease" by doctors who wanted it to be taken seriously—had been built in a lab. It had come on so quickly, they said, and it had spread so fast.

There was no evidence that Morris's disease was an act of bioterrorism. No group stepped forward to claim it, an absence which inflamed the conspiracy theorists even further. After all, the first reported cases had been in Orlando, Florida—most notably Lisa Morris, age eight, whose death had earned her the position of "index case"—but they had been followed by infections all over the world. Any terrorist group foolish enough to work with one of the most infectious diseases known to man would quickly have learned the error of their ways as their own children and elders began to sicken and die. Someone claiming responsibility for the outbreak would almost have proven that it *wasn't* an act of bioterrorism.

It didn't really matter whether Morris's disease was manmade or not. It was a killer either way.

It began like measles: with a fever, a runny nose, a sore throat, all the little signs the human body uses to signal that something is wrong, that perhaps the time for precautions has come and gone, fading uselessly into the distance, one more missed opportunity in the rearview mirror of a lifetime. From there, it progressed to Koplik's spots inside the mouth, small and white and possible to overlook—and most importantly, *ordinary*. At the second stage, it still looked enough like ordinary measles to be dismissed as a consequence of weakening herd immunity brought on by a growing anti-vaccination movement.

Morris's disease began to shine in the third stage. The characteristic measles rash appeared, as expected, on the fourth or fifth day after the start of symptoms. But rather than going through the usual darkening phase, it continued to worsen, softening and weakening the skin, until every motion of a Morris's victim risked tearing and infection. Brain inflammation, relatively uncommon in measles victims, occurred in up to thirty percent of cases. Exact numbers were difficult to determine. People died too quickly to be sure of what, precisely, the disease had done to kill them.

Lisa.

On her first day of full infectious latency, the first day when she was capable of spreading the disease to others, Lisa Morris lied to her parents, saying her slight unsteadiness was a result of not sleeping well. Her mother felt her forehead and noted that she was running a low fever, but Lisa was so excited over the idea of one more day at the amusement park, and the tickets had already been paid for; the big entertainment conglomerates didn't make a habit of refunding costs because of a sick child. What kind of business model would that have been?

"She's fine," said Lisa's mother.

"All right," said Lisa's father.

Lisa, fighting a losing battle against the disease that would be her namesake and only legacy, said nothing, but drank her orange juice in small sips, grimacing as it burned her throat, and hoped neither of them would try to make her eat breakfast.

The Morris family boarded the complimentary bus service outside their resort. It contained thirteen children, twenty-nine adults heading for the amusement park, the driver, and three custodial workers in street clothes. Lisa coughed eighteen times while she was on the bus. Despite covering her mouth, she infected nine of the children and fifteen of the adults, including the driver and all three custodial workers. The droplets of her saliva containing the virus would hover in the air at the center of the vehicle for almost an hour, continuing to spread the infection long after the Morris family had moved on. That single voyage would be responsible, directly or indirectly, for almost a hundred primary infections. Each of those people would go on to infect hundreds more. The outbreak was beyond control long before anyone realized it was happening.

The Morris family proceeded from the bus to the amusement park, where they spent the day standing in lines, eating in themed restaurants, and riding attractions, many of which took place in enclosed spaces with little outside air. The roller coasters were too fast to present an infection risk...but Lisa touched the safety harnesses and the grip bars and the sides of the cars, and everything she touched retained a layer of skin cells, mucus, and viral particles. The number of primary cases mounted throughout the day. None of the infected—the victims, the carriers, the statistics of the initial outbreak—would show symptoms until later in the week. Many of them would continue to leave their homes even as they began feeling unwell. The virus would spread.

The virus always spreads. Despite the work of epidemiologists around the world—those who survived the first wave of Morris's disease, and the second, and the third; those who didn't get pulled away by other, more pressing projects—were never able to determine exactly how Lisa Morris was exposed. She was the first to die; she was only one of a number of seemingly spontaneous cases traced back to the Orlando area. Those who spoke about the matter at all claimed that the disease's sudden appearance supported the idea of it having been manmade...but no one wanted to hear that. No one wanted to consider the fact that we might, in the end, have done this to ourselves.

At the end of the day, the Morris family returned to their hotel. On the way, Lisa infected the riders on their return bus journey, one of the bellhops in the lobby, and the woman at the front desk who gave her a piece of hard candy for her throat. She infected two passing families on their way to the shuttle stop for their ride to the airport. She did all this unwittingly, unknowingly, with no intent to do harm. Lisa Morris was a sweet child whose only crime was one that every eight-year-old had the potential to willingly commit: concealing an illness so as not to miss what seemed like a once-in-a-lifetime opportunity.

It was. There would be no more vacations for Lisa Morris, no more amusement parks, no more summers in the sun. Her father was also about to lose those things, but he had been able to experience more of them before he went; his death, while no less a tragedy, would be weighted more lightly by the scales of the historians who tried, in their awkward, stuttering way, to chronicle the beginnings of the outbreak.

In the morning, the Morris family checked out of their hotel, boarded the shuttle, and rode to the airport. The number of infections stemming from these simple actions have never been calculated. Nor has the number of infections which began as they wound their way through security, as they boarded the plane, as they flew home.

Aunt Isabelle was waiting at baggage claim, holding a large construction paper sign that read "Lisa!!!!—and those other people too (I guess)." She was still wearing her white coat from working at the clinic, and Lisa, who was feeling very bad by that point, so bad that her vision was getting fuzzy around the edges, like she was looking through a plate of agar jelly, found the strength to run to her. She flung her arms around her beloved aunt's ribcage, her beloved aunt who had given her all her vaccinations and performed all her checkups, who she associated with health and healing and getting better, and tried to wish her sick away.

Lisa's parents, who had had plenty of time during their cross-country flight to observe the progression of her symptoms, followed more slowly. Her father was already starting to feel unwell, a combination of headache and vague dizziness that he attributed to jetlag and the dry air of the plane. He coughed once as he walked. Because he was not sick, merely worn-down from travel and from looking after an ailing child, he did not think to cover his mouth. Of such small moments are disasters made.

Aunt Isabelle—known to most of her patients as "Dr. Gauley"—touched her niece's forehead with the back of her hand and frowned sharply. "You're burning up," she said.

"Hello to you, too, Izzy," said her sister. Brooke Morris looked as exhausted as her husband. Unlike her husband, she otherwise felt fine. A culture of her blood would have shown no viral bodies, slumbering or otherwise. Her immune system, detecting the first invaders, had been successful at repelling them, a quick, brutal battle that had happened entirely below the level of her consciousness. In a world under microscopic siege, she had somehow managed to close her own biological borders before the invasion could properly begin. It was a victory she would soon come to regret, when the funerals began.

"Sorry," said Izzy, not sounding sorry in the least. "I'm serious, though. She's burning up. I told you those theme parks were hotbeds of disease." *I told you not to go. Oh, God, I told you not to go.* "How long has she been like this?"

"She started feeling a little punky yesterday, didn't you, princess?" said Lisa's dad. In the end, he would outlive her by a handful of hours, fighting to breathe through the tube in his throat, no longer capable of forming coherent thoughts. The last sound he heard would be his wife, weeping into her hands, and the distant beeping of the machinery that had tried, and failed, to keep him alive. By the time he died, it would be a mercy.

Lisa, her face pressed to Aunt Isabelle's shirt, didn't answer. Her head was spinning. She wasn't sure she could speak.

The way Lisa's neck was bent gave Izzy a look down the tented fabric of her shirt, to what should have been the smooth skin of her back. It was covered in a deep red, vicious-looking rash, humped up in little peaks, like goosebumps, like acne. For a moment—a moment she'd be ashamed of for the rest of her life—Izzy wanted to shove her niece away from her, to run and douse herself in antiseptic, to scrub and scrub and scrub until there was no trace of infection remaining.

Florida. They'd gone to fucking *Florida*.

Instead of pushing Lisa away, Izzy swallowed her fear, took a deep breath, and said, "Rick, can you please take care of the bags and call an Uber to get you home? Lisa and I have to go to the office. Brooke should come."

Rick opened his mouth to protest, and froze when he saw the look on his sister-in-law's face, that scrambled mixture of fear and determination. Slowly, he nodded.

"All right," he said.

"Thank you," said Izzy. She scooped her niece into her arms, the heat baking off the little girl's body so strong that she wanted to scream, to rage, to demand how they could possibly have missed it long enough to make it all the way home. She wanted to shout at them for taking the little girl to Florida in the first place. She'd warned Brooke about what a hotbed of infection those amusement parks were, how anyone who wanted a disease to spread could...

Could...

There wasn't time to dwell on who had and hadn't listened. Izzy walked until they were out of the airport, Brooke trailing behind her, too worried to ask questions. When they reached the parking garage, Izzy broke into a run.

It's measles, it has to be, she thought. *It's just measles, she's had her vaccinations, she'll be fine, it's just measles. Anything else would be so improbable it wouldn't—it's just measles.* The disease had complications, yes, but they were manageable, especially with immediate medical care. Isolating and quarantining Lisa before she became the focal point of a California outbreak was what mattered now. A spike of irritation forced its way through her panic, and she shoved it aside. There would be time to be furious later, when Lisa was stabilized.

By the time they reached the hospital associated with her pediatric practice, Lisa had slipped into a feverish sleep, muttering to herself and flinching when touched. Her fever was peaking, rendering her hot to the touch, and her nose was running almost constantly. Izzy had called ahead. They were met at the door by a group of residents, wheeling a cot with an isolation barrier already in place around it. They wheeled Lisa into the hospital, Izzy and Brooke following, heading for quarantine.

Lisa was officially diagnosed with measles two hours after her flight home from Florida touched down. She was pronounced stable just before midnight, with her mother standing by, white-knuckled and terrified, blaming herself for every sign she had missed, for every sneeze of every child in the entire state of Florida. She fell asleep next to her daughter's bed somewhere around three o'clock in the morning, her sister holding tightly to her hand.

She woke alone, to the sound of blaring machines and a series of increasingly disjointed text messages on her phone, her husband chronicling the progression of his own symptoms and his decision to admit himself to the hospital.

Lisa died at ten minutes past six in the morning, the first victim of what was initially identified as measles encephalitis, and would later be known as Morris's encephalitis, and still later as Morris's disease, a questionable, terrible form of immortality.

If there is any mercy in this story, it is that she did not suffer when she reached the end.

She was no longer there to understand what suffering was.

3.

ACCORDING TO the official records, the initial wave of the American Morris's disease epidemic began with the first identified case: Lisa Morris, age eight. That wave ended six months later, when sixteen-month-old Thomas Wheeler became ill following a trip to the local grocery store. In the end, more than thirty million presented clear symptoms of the disease, with an estimated additional seventeen million becoming subclinical carriers. Of the thirty million who sickened, ten million died, offering the most substantial deviation from traditional measles, which has a much lower fatality rate.

Ten million graves; ten million empty beds. The figure was not exact, might never be exact, might never catch every victim who fell through the net of social services and medical treatment. It didn't need to. It was too big to require precision: it could shock and horrify enough by merely existing, imprecise and inarguable, filling the entire sky.

Morris's was not restricted to America. Morris's was a virus, capable of traveling at the speed of air travel, spreading silently for days before Lisa Morris spiked a fever and revealed the presence of a killer. An estimated ten to fifteen percent of the world's overall population was infected by Morris's before the first wave of the epidemic ended. An estimated five percent died. The number of lives lost exceeded any manmade crisis, any act of terrorism, any war.

Still, no one claimed responsibility. Still, no one stood up and said "this was me, this was my work, this was my doing; this is what I wanted." Everyone agreed that Morris's disease was the work of a human hand: it had to be. It did its job too quickly, too well, and without a hint of hesitation. A virus, after all, has no morality, no capacity for sorrow.

The graves were filled, when they could be; the bodies were burned, when the graves weren't enough. Prayers were said. Accusations were levied against everyone from the CDC to the anti-vaccination movement to the Department of Homeland Security. Parents became hyper-aware of every cough and sneeze, herding their children away from potential sources of infection like they could somehow keep disease away through sheer force of will. For a short time, every child who came to Dr. Gauley's office received a full course of vaccinations, their parents white-knuckled and terrified and listening to her every recommendation...at least until the vaccinations ran out, and the factories that made them collapsed under the weight of the demand.

And over it all hung the feeling that another shoe was preparing, somehow, to drop.

The shoe dropped six months after the death of Thomas Wheeler. It began with a single case of whooping cough.

Whooping cough is not a pleasant illness, if such things can be said to truly exist. Named for the sound its struggling victims make as they try to inhale, it can bring on spasms of coughing severe enough to break ribs. It can leave permanent scarring of the larynx, esophagus, and vocal chords. It can kill. Like measles—true measles—it had always been a disease which claimed a certain number of casualties, but whose targets would, in the main, recover.

Not this time. The whooping cough outbreak following Morris's disease was the most severe the modern world had ever seen. It spread like wildfire, showing the gaps in the world's recently enhanced quarantine protocols, and by the time the coughing faded into a wheezing whimper, thousands more were dead, both among the known survivors of Morris's and the formerly invisible subclinical survivors. More graves were filled. More bodies were burned.

When the mumps reappeared, no one was honestly surprised.

Scientists had known for some time that the true danger of a measles outbreak would not be the measles themselves, but the strange "forgetfulness" of the human immune system following exposure. A person who had survived measles would lose some measure of their preexisting immunity to other diseases, whether that immunity had been acquired through natural or manmade means. By waltzing across the world, Morris's disease had, effectively, rendered the entire population unvaccinated, and now the terrible consequences of that reality were being revealed.

More people died. The brief window of obedience to medical recommendations slammed shut, leaving terrified parents on one side and desperate doctors on the other, both wanting nothing more than the best for their children, both trying to save lives.

Both, in their own ways, in this terrible moment, failing.

Lisa Morris was dead.

All the rest came after.

2: | Transcription

1.

"MURDERER!"

The voice was unfamiliar; the water balloon flying toward her was not. Izzy ducked, lowering her umbrella so the projectile burst against it rather than against her face. That would have been wonderful, if it hadn't opened the floodgates. At least a dozen more water balloons hit the umbrella with sickening pops before her escorts could hurry back from the door, grab her elbows, and guide her gently into the clinic.

The shouting from outside became muted when the doors closed, locking the three of them safely inside the lobby. Two guards quickly moved through the waiting area, checking the ID cards and appointments of the waiting parents, all of whom looked sickened and disturbed by the chaos outside. Not a single person attempted to stand or leave. They had come to the vaccination clinic out of desperation, and after braving the gauntlet outside, there was no way they were going to move for anything short of a fire.

Maybe not even for that. Izzy looked at her umbrella, dripping with what she sincerely hoped was artificial blood, and suspected that many of these parents would continue rolling up their children's sleeves even as the flames approached, choosing a temporary risk over one which they viewed—not incorrectly—as having much greater potential impact.

One of the nurses appeared and whisked the umbrella away. Izzy switched her silent gaze to the clinic walls. This had been a bright, friendly place once, with windows shielded only by gauzy curtains designed to improve client privacy, with shelves full of books with colorful covers on the outside and colorful characters on the inside, with chests of toys. The toys were still there, but they were battered now, rendered old before their time by constant, aggressive sterilization. Plush had always been frowned upon. Now it was the sort of thing that had to be thrown away immediately, too fragile to survive the decontamination protocols.

Izzy understood how that felt.

"Dr. Gauley?"

She turned, snapping out of her reverie and pasting a smile on her face before the gesture finished. Her clients liked it when she smiled. It made them feel like this was all temporary, somehow, like the world was going to wake up one morning and get back to normal. "Yes?"

The woman behind her was neat, in the way of people who had come straight from an office job of some kind. She was wearing a bright yellow Parent Alert bracelet on her left wrist, its display blinking a steady, soothing green. Most parents set the default screen to that blinking green, preferring the constant "my child is fine" beacon to the more granular invasion of privacy that was pulse, temperature, hydration level. The Parent Alert was increasing in popularity all the time. It couldn't *really* predict a child's health, not without the ability to test their blood for infections and viruses, but it could provide that reassuring list of statistics, that soothing green glow, and for many parents, that was more than enough.

"Ah," said Izzy, recognizing the woman. "Hello, Carla. What can I do for you today? Do you have an appointment?" In theory her clinic didn't take walk-ins unless it was an emergency, and in most emergency cases, would recommend the child be taken directly to the hospital. That rule was from the days before Morris's. These days, anything that allowed her to practice medicine—and maybe more importantly, keep the lights on a little longer—was likely to be allowed.

Sometimes Izzy suspected the only reason she was still practicing at all was that Brooke had never gone through with her long-muttered plan to divorce Rick and return to her maiden name. If it had been Gauley's disease, not Morris's, there was no way the clinic would have survived. That suspicion was always followed by memories of Lisa, and by so much shame that she thought she might break under the weight of it.

Sometimes she thought it might have been better if her own divorce had never gone through, if her past and her present hadn't been so neatly segmented. If she'd still been Dr. Isabella Charles, virologist and expert, and not Dr. Isabella Gauley, pediatrician and cog in the struggling machine of post-Morris's public health.

"It's Michael," said the woman, pitching her voice lower, as if she feared her son might hear her. As for the boy himself, he was focused entirely on his hand-held video game system, tuning out the room around him with an expert's skill. Izzy envied him that, more than a little. "He seems under the weather. I didn't want him going back to that school until I knew he was all right."

"That" school was one of the finest middle schools in the district, with a strict presentee policy for unwell children and an excellent system of remote classroom options. Izzy kept smiling pleasantly. "Do you have an appointment?" she repeated.

"Ah." The woman's gaze turned shifty. "Not…exactly, but since we're such good clients of yours, I was hoping you'd be able to fit us in today."

"Of course we can," said Izzy, sighing inwardly. Another day without a chance to sit down and eat a proper lunch. "You'll have to wait until I've got a gap in my schedule, though. I can't move people when it's not an emergency."

Again, that shifty look. Izzy braced herself. Carla Daniels had a tendency to think that the smallest sniffle on the part of her beloved son was more important than a broken arm in any other child. Izzy couldn't entirely blame her. Carla was another of the unlucky ones who'd lost multiple people from her immediate family—in Carla's case, both her teenage daughters had succumbed, Sherry to Morris's disease, and Tina, who had managed to survive the first disease with minimal complications, to whooping cough. It was no surprise that the woman treated her surviving child like he was made of glass. It would have been more of a surprise if she hadn't.

Finally, Carla sighed. "No," she said. "It's not an emergency. We'll wait."

"Thank you," said Izzy, and started for the door next to the reception window. The offices and exam rooms were on the other side. Once it was locked behind her, she'd have one more layer of safety between her and the outside world.

She made it a habit to ease the door closed—a habit one of her nurse practitioners disrupted when he pushed past her, letting the door slam. The sound was enough like a gunshot to set her heart racing and make her breath catch in her throat, until she felt like an engine on the verge of exploding. She staggered, bracing herself against the wall as she tried to work through the mindfulness exercises that would bring her pulse back down. Passing members of her staff shot her sympathetic looks, but didn't interfere. The sight of Dr. Isabelle Gauley, renowned pediatrician and vaccination advocate, on the verge of a panic attack had become all too common lately.

According to her therapist—healer, heal thyself—her responses to traumatic stimuli were entirely natural, considering what she'd been through. She wasn't the only medical professional to suffer PTSD in the aftermath of Morris's disease. The only reason she was still practicing, the only reason *any* of them were still practicing, was that so many had been struck down that there was no room for the survivors to stop. She had to stay in practice. She had to keep trying to save the children who had survived. If she didn't, if she couldn't, who would?

"You breathing yet, or should I come back in five minutes?"

Izzy looked up. Her head nurse was looking at her with his usual mixture of sympathy and impatience, a blend that seemed to have been specifically designed for his face. No one else could project "I love you but I sort of want to shake you right now" the way Mark could. The tattoos helped. He was a big, burly man with tattoos on his neck, arms, and hands, bold black lines against brown skin, and people who saw them before they saw *him* usually assumed he was so much tougher than he actually was.

Sandy—one of the other nurses, a Japanese-American woman whose vices were mostly Hello Kitty-related, possibly as a way of distinguishing herself from her adoptive Mormon family—had asked him once why he didn't get them all lasered off. The disaster pay for pediatric nurses was still in place, and the ones who kept showing up for work were making more money than most of them had ever expected to see in their lives. Laser tattoo removal would have been a drop in the bucket. Mark had laughed and said that if he didn't want to have his tattoos, he wouldn't have paid to get them, and that had been the end of that.

Izzy thought if Sandy and Mark could get along, there might be hope for humanity after all. Not a lot of hope, but hope, all the same.

"Sorry," she said, not pushing herself away from the wall. "Bad day."

"Asshole with the water balloons outside again, huh?"

Mark never said anything carelessly. By swearing, he was reminding her that there were no children in the exam room area. There were no children because she had yet to start seeing them. Meaning their scheduled patients and their walk-ins would be stacking up outside, and if they allowed that to continue, some of them would start leaving, sick children or not. Hospitals and medical waiting rooms were some of the best places to catch the latest and greatest diseases, and there were so *many* diseases.

Morris's disease had been like an EMP for child and adult immune systems alike, forcing the revaccination of a horrifying percentage of the population—and not everyone was willing to listen when asked to see their doctor about getting another round of shots. The debates in Washington raged on, trying to find the line between bodily autonomy and societal good, and in the meantime, places like this, offices like this, had to keep the children breathing.

"I'm ready," said Izzy. She took a deep breath, and straightened. "Bring in my first appointment."

2.

THE LOGIC of the picketers outside Dr. Gauley's practice was terribly easy to follow, if she let go of the idea that words had meanings, and chose instead to go down the rabbit hole of correlation equaling causation.

The anti-vaccination movement had managed to survive Morris's disease, thanks to the one-two punch of vaccinated children dying and vaccine stockpiles running out across the country and the world as governments struggled to break the back of the disease. When the secondary epidemics had begun, certain groups had seen it as their opportunity to come out of the shadows and start peddling their unique brand of poison once again. So many vaccinated children had died, they said; so many people who had supposedly been protected by the great god Science had fallen. How could that be anything but proof that vaccination was a scam advocated by greedy doctors who just wanted that sweet cash from the big pharmacy companies? The proof was in the payoff.

(Never mind that vaccines were some of the least profitable products a pharmaceutical company had. Never mind that a successful vaccine closed the door to dozens of treatments, medicines and aftercare and even lifetime dependencies on certain drugs. The best thing "Big Pharma" could have done for their bottom line would have been discontinuing vaccination altogether. The fact that they hadn't proved that there were still some people, if not enough, who valued the public good over their profit margins.)

Attempting to educate the furious and the frightened about herd immunity, and how the first wave of the anti-vaccination movement's success had been what actually opened the door for Morris's disease to come dancing through, had been a failure. No one wanted to look at the body of their dead child—and there were so many dead children, so impossibly many dead children— and hear that they had done this, either directly or by saying "oh, that's just their way" about a sibling or friend who refused to vaccinate. Herd immunity had always been, would always be, so impossibly fragile. It needed all the help it could get.

The anti-vaccination movement had received a massive boost from an unexpected source: the pro-choice movement, acting in response to a move by some politically canny members of their opposite number. Abortion rights in America had always hinged partially on the concept of bodily autonomy: the idea that an individual could not be forced to give up control of their body for the duration of a pregnancy simply because they happened to have been born in possession of a functional womb. Bodily autonomy also stated that people could not be forced to become organ donors...or to be vaccinated. Refusing certain basic services to unvaccinated individuals had always been allowed, on a state by state basis, but in the aftermath of Morris's disease, more and more people had begun to demand the exclusion of the unvaccinated from society.

Exceptions would be made for those with medical reasons to refuse vaccination, of course, people with autoimmune disorders, people who were undergoing chemotherapy. Humanity's most vulnerable, who could not receive the life-saving shots, who depended upon herd immunity to keep them breathing. Everyone else, however, needed to form a living wall around their fellows. No more religious exemptions. No more personal exemptions.

No more bodily autonomy.

It might have been possible to craft legislation precise enough to thread the needle, explaining that in this case, the risk to the health of others outweighed the need to maintain the sanctity of skin, the communion of consent. A surprising number of individuals had no interest in threading that needle. They wanted bodily autonomy erased in a single legislative stroke, opening the door to outlawing all forms of abortion. After all, if forcibly vaccinating children to save their lives was allowable under the law, shouldn't saving the lives of the unborn fall into the same bucket?

The fight raged on, while the anti-vaccination movement howled about how they refused to be seen as baby killers simply because they wanted the right to decide whether their children had poison pumped into their bodies, and the pro-vaccination movement squirmed and twisted and tried to figure out how they had wound up on the right side and the wrong side of history at the same time.

(The families that had lost children to Morris's disease lined up for their vaccinations every time the scarce supply became available, sleeves rolled up, arms held out, like they were looking for salvation in the tip of a needle, like they believed they could rebuild herd immunity all by themselves, like they could avenge the dead. Izzy blessed them with every strained breath, and worked to keep immunizing their children against a dozen diseases that should never have been a problem, not in this world, not after everything they'd already gone through to save themselves.)

Izzy stepped into the exam room, a clipboard already in her hands, ready to go through the receiving patter she had performed a thousand times before. Most of the real work was done by her nurses, who gave shots, took vitals, and distributed basic medications with deft hands. She would have been lost without them. But people wanted to see a doctor. It made them feel safe. She was the one with the degrees on her wall, after all, and since she wanted them to keep coming back, to keep letting her take care of their children, she didn't argue.

"All right," she said. "It says here that your little girl is running a fever—"

"She was, at the end," said Angela.

Izzy froze.

Angela was perched on the paper-swathed bed they used for patient exams, her feet hanging a foot or so above the ground. Everyone looked like a child when they sat on one of those tables, young and fragile and all too breakable. Her clothes didn't help. She wore a sweater several sizes too large for her, her slender torso swimming in layers of wool, and a shapeless skirt that turned her legs into a dark gray puddle, like something left by the side of the road.

"You've lost weight," blurted Izzy. She blanched. "I didn't mean that. I mean, I meant that. You look like hell. I mean...I don't know what I mean. What are you doing here?"

"You haven't been answering my email," said Angela. "I wanted to see at least one of my sisters, and Brooke hasn't spoken to me since the funeral."

"I've been busy, and Brooke has other things on her mind. I assume Mark snuck you in here?" When Angela nodded, Izzy sighed. "He thinks I work too hard. He probably figured we'd be so excited to see each other that we'd leave right away for coffee or something and give me an hour's peace. Which doesn't get the appointments finished or the kids seen, but hey, at least I'd have *coffee*."

Angela raised an eyebrow. "I don't think I've ever heard someone say 'coffee' like it meant 'bullshit' before."

"I've been having a hard month."

"You're not the only one."

Silence.

"Lisa's birthday was last week."

"I know." Izzy had purchased a cake, had blown up balloons and held a small party, just her and a picture of Lisa from that last vacation, smiling forever, frozen at eight years old, never changing, never growing up, never growing old. One more little girl for the shores of Never-Never Land.

"You could have called."

"No. I really couldn't have."

"You could at least—"

"You went on the news and told everyone who'd listen—and that's a lot of people these days, Angela, that's a *lot* of people— that you supported suspension of bodily autonomy until we could confirm the eradication of all known infectious disease. Which means forever. You understand that, don't you? There's a reason I wasn't on that broadcast. There's a reason *Brooke* wasn't on that broadcast."

"She was my daughter too!"

"No, she wasn't. You signed the adoption papers, remember? It doesn't matter whose body she grew inside, she was *Brooke's* daughter, and Brooke understands that we can't trade the future of every potential parent for an idea of safety that's not going to work! I want people to *choose* vaccination, for themselves and their children, absolutely. It's the right decision. It protects everyone. But we can't make it mandatory. We'll never be able to enforce it."

"We made seatbelts mandatory."

Izzy pinched the bridge of her nose. She could already feel the headache forming there, a dull, looming pain that spoke of a difficult afternoon to come. "Seatbelts don't enter your body. They sit outside of it. They don't violate bodily autonomy."

"I thought you cared about children."

"And I thought you were more interested in picketing my practice than coming inside it." Izzy dropped her hand and glared. "That's what you really told Mark, isn't it? That you wanted to talk to me about calling off your damned dogs? Well, talk. Tell me what it takes to make them all go away."

For the first time, Angela looked faintly uncomfortable. "I don't think I could break up the protest if I wanted to," she admitted. "It's taken on a life of its own at this point. People are very passionate about the topic of childhood vaccination."

"Then why…" Izzy stopped. Her eyes narrowed. "Get out."

"Please, Izzy, if you'd just *listen*, you'd understand what we're trying to do. We need you. And you need us! Once this passes, the vaccination clinics are going to be huge. We're going to need every hand we can possibly get. And they'll *pay*. This could make us both rich. People still listen to you. They respect you." Something in Angela's tone told Izzy that her sister didn't know *why* people respected Izzy. Only that they did.

Only that it could be used.

"Get out," repeated Izzy. "Get out, and if you *ever* talk your way in here again, I will have you arrested. Do I make myself clear? If you come anywhere near me, or Brooke, you will go to prison."

Angela's expression hardened. "Still think you're better than anyone else, don't you, Isabelle? Couldn't save your own sister's kid. Couldn't save any of those kids. How many bodies did you burn to keep people from realizing how high the numbers were?" She slid off the table, eyes burning with a bright, fanatic flame. "If you're not with us, you're against us. Don't forget that."

She whipped out of the room in a swirl of skirt and sweater that was probably meant to be dramatic, but was really and simply sad. Izzy sagged, catching herself against the wall as she took a moment to breathe. Then she pulled out her phone.

The Gauley sisters—how they had loved that label when they were children, three girls against the big, bright world! How they had treasured it—had had the good fortune to be born to wealthy parents who saw to their every childhood need, reasoning, as many parents do, that adulthood would be the time for them to learn independence and privation. While they were young, they'd had the best of everything. The best teachers, the best tutors, the best extracurricular activities. None of them had turned out particularly athletic, but they had still been offered ballet, horseback riding lessons, tennis, whatever had struck their fancies. As long as they took their opportunities seriously, more opportunities would always be offered.

Isabelle, the eldest, had been fascinated by biology from the time she was a very small child. Somehow, the classes she was offered and the choices she made had led her toward pre-med, and then to medical school, where she had met her eventual husband and found what she had believed to be her calling: virology. But castles built on clouds have a way of crashing to earth, and when that castle had fallen down, she had been forced to rebuild under her maiden name, going into pediatrics. Her parents had paid for the building where her first practice had been opened, but everything since then had been her. Her mind, her money, her hard work. She was an American success story, and while she understood that it had been easier for her because of where she'd started, she had done all the hard work on her own.

Brooke, the youngest, had looked at her scientifically-minded elder sister and dreamt of finding a way to turn science to her own ends. She had tinkered and she had toyed and then she had discovered chemistry, and she had never once looked back. The interplay of molecules and compounds was her delight. She had a steady hand and a flexible mind, and when she had decided that pharmacy school was the right choice for her, her parents had been there with their checkbooks in their hands, ready to do whatever they could to support her dreams. Unlike her sister, she didn't open her own practice. There wasn't much demand for independent pharmacists, and she'd never wanted to be anyone's boss. So she'd gone to work for a large pharmacy, making good money and leaving her with time for the child she had always so desperately wanted, the child she had never been able to conceive on her own.

Enter Angela. The middle child, neither ambitious nor determined. Smart, yes. As smart as either of her sisters, if not smarter, in her wild, undisciplined way. She had been a compass searching for her version of true north ever since they were children. In her quest, she had stumbled into one form of activism after another— not a bad thing, especially not with her brain and her ceaseless energy, but not a good thing either. She couldn't fight for animal rights without breaking into labs and releasing the test animals in the middle of the night, heedless of whether some of those animals might already have been infected with one unspeakable virus or another, or whether those animals would even be able to survive in the wild. She couldn't campaign against meat without setting fire to a family farm, killing more animals than her earlier activism had freed. Her heart was in the right place. Her causes weren't bad ones. She just refused to consider the logical consequences of her actions.

When she had shown up on Izzy's doorstep five months pregnant and asking her sister to help her arrange an adoption of the baby she couldn't keep but couldn't bring herself to lose, Izzy had thought of Brooke, thought of failed pregnancy tests and tears over afternoon coffee. She had thought of the old adage that some things were best kept in the family. And she wasn't sorry. Even now, on the other side of everything, with Lisa in the ground and Brooke broken in a subtle but absolute way, Izzy couldn't be sorry. They'd been given eight years of Lisa, wonderful, witty, wild Lisa, who could have been anything at all, would have been everything, if not for Morris's disease. If not for the terrible timing of everything.

Izzy pushed herself away from the wall, sucking in a lungful of air so bitter that it burned, and opened the door.

Mark was standing right outside. "I'm sorry," he said. "She said—"

"I know my sister," said Izzy. "Send in my next patient."

3.

THE REST of the day was blissfully unremarkable. Izzy saw patients, some new, some familiar. She diagnosed conditions and ordered tests and prescribed medications, some of which would be compounded at Brooke's pharmacy, depending on the insurance of the parents. She recommended courses of vaccination, explaining the minimal risks and the benefits to both the child and their community.

"Herd immunity," she said, over and over again, until she wanted to scream. "It's all about building herd immunity."

That was the hardest thing to understand, in the aftermath of Morris's disease, in a world where everyone had seen what happened if they didn't have a way to break the back of an epidemic. They *knew*. They had to know. It had been on every news outlet, in every paper, on every website. Herd immunity was the key to surviving so many of the things the world had to throw at humanity, and without it, they were all simply playing roulette with their lives. Not just their lives: the lives of others. A single vaccination wouldn't change what was coming. It would take the world stepping up, *voluntarily*, to lessen the danger.

Some parents listened, rolled up their sleeves along with their children's, took the prick of the needle and the risk of mild swelling or fever without hesitation. Some parents understood.

Some didn't.

Izzy stepped into the small break room with her head bowed, her hair a frizzy corona of strawberry blonde curls and tangles. No matter how hard she tried, she could never seem to keep it under control for an entire shift. Lisa had shared the same hair.

Dammit. Lisa. She should never have gotten sick. If she hadn't gone to that damn amusement park, if her parents had listened and kept her out of Florida, if only, if only...

"Dr. Gauley? You all right?"

Izzy's head snapped up. She stared at Sandy. Sandy looked sympathetically back.

"Long day?" she asked.

"You could say that," said Izzy wearily. "Is there any coffee left? I might violate the Geneva Convention for a cup of coffee. Not decaf. Decaf doesn't deserve the name."

"I keep telling you we should get one of those machines that can make a cup of whatever you want in sixty seconds."

"And I keep telling you that they're bad for the environment."

Sandy scoffed. "Please. One little coffee pod machine isn't going to be what brings this house of cards toppling down. You want me to go outside and squirt protestors with a hose again? Watching them run off all angry and wet always makes you feel better."

"Mark let Angela in here."

To Sandy's credit, she didn't drop the cup she was holding, merely scowled and asked, "Did he hit his head? Does he *want* to?"

"No," said Izzy. "He still thinks we can convince her to call off her dogs."

"Please." Sandy rolled her eyes heavenward. "That woman never met a cause that she didn't want to ride into the ground, and this one here's the big brass bell. She's in the news, she's becoming a martyr and a figurehead at the same time, and it's all on the back of a little girl she only ever saw on Christmas and Thanksgiving. You think she's ever told her band of fools how many birthday parties she missed?"

"Brooke invited her," said Izzy.

"And yet she didn't come."

"Yeah." There were a few inches of dark liquid left in the bottom of the coffee pot. Izzy picked it up, shook it, and dumped its contents into her cup, where they pooled unappealingly. "Caffeine's a poison, you know."

"That's why I don't drink it," said Sandy. "Kick the habit. Get that monkey off your back and join me in glorious purity."

"You drink beer."

"Because I'm not Mormon anymore. And if I needed beer to get through the day the way everyone around here needs coffee, you'd call for an intervention, or just fire me. Firing seems more likely, all things considered. Now what are we going to do about that sister of yours? Want me to talk to Mark?"

"I already did. He's promised never to do it again."

Sandy looked at her with solemn concern. "Do you believe him?"

"I do, mostly because I threatened to fire him if he ever pulled that sort of stunt again, no matter how well-intentioned." Izzy poured cream and sugar into her coffee, diluting it until it looked like it might actually be drinkable. "He wants things to get better. He's scared. He's also doing a vaccination clinic in Fremont tonight. They need more nurses who speak Spanish. It's hard enough to convince people to vaccinate without a language barrier getting in the way."

"At least he's still trying to fix the world."

"Aren't we all?"

Izzy stayed in the kitchen, sipping her coffee, while the rest of the staff packed up their things and went home. They left in small groups, two at a time, heading out the back door with their hands on their purses and their wallets, with their phones set to speed dial the police if they said the correct code words. Somehow, coming to the clinic had become as dangerous as walking into a tiger's den. Sooner or later, someone was going to get seriously hurt.

Eventually, the coffee ran out, and Izzy started to think of following her staff out; of heading home to her small, empty apartment, with the blank spots on the walls where Lisa's pictures had been, before she'd taken them all down in a fit of grief and rage. She almost never had company anyway; there was no one to notice their absence, or wonder what it meant.

Her phone rang. The number was blocked. That wasn't so unusual. The people who wanted to spit unimaginative death threats in her ears were remarkably good at getting hold of her number, and they had learned not to let her see where they were calling from, since *she* was remarkably good at calling the police. It would have been better not to answer them. She knew that, and she answered anyway. Call it the only form of penance she had left.

"Might be worth a laugh," she muttered, and swiped her thumb across the screen, raising the phone to her ear. "Hello?"

"Izzy? It's Brooke. I need you."

Izzy nearly dropped the phone.

4.

LISA MORRIS had been lucky, in some ways: she had died early enough that the funeral homes hadn't been completely overwhelmed by the number of bodies stacking up in the morgues, piled in hallways and even left on sidewalks in hopes that someone would come along and take care of them. Her mother had been able to arrange for a proper burial for her, laying her to rest alongside her grandparents, and her father, who had followed her too quickly into the earth.

(Izzy wondered, as she walked along the cemetery path, whether Lisa's biological father even knew she was gone. He was aware of her existence, had voluntarily signed the papers severing his parental rights, and he had been a perfect gentleman about the entire process, throwing up no barriers, presenting no unnecessary complications. But she thought that if she had known about a child, somewhere out there in the world, she would have wanted to keep track of them, at least a little. At least enough to know if they were dead. So far as she knew, no one had called him to come to Lisa's funeral. She wanted to be sorry about that. Somehow, all she could find the strength to be was numb.)

As she approached Lisa's grave, a figure came into view, standing next to the headstone, shoulders bowed, one hand extended to touch the marble. It was like a scene out of a morbid Norman Rockwell painting, and Izzy felt obscurely like she was intruding, like this was a moment that had never been meant for her. She kept on walking anyway. There was only so much time before the sun went down and the cemetery gates were locked for the evening. Better to get this over with.

"Brooke."

Her sister lifted her head. Her hair, a few shades darker than Izzy's or Lisa's, was messy, like it hadn't been brushed before she pulled it back into a sloppy ponytail. There was lipstick on her upper lip, but not her lower. Chewing her lip was a nervous tic she'd had since they were kids. She'd seemed to have it under control for a while. Izzy supposed the death of her husband and daughter in the same week was good enough reason to backslide.

"You came," said Brooke, looking relieved. "Did you remember to leave your phone in the car?

"I did, and I came," Izzy agreed. Seeing both her sisters in the same day was strange to the point of becoming almost physically painful, sending tingles over her skin. It itched. "What was so important that I had to meet you here?"

"Have you been visiting Lisa?"

Izzy looked away.

"You promised me."

"I feel...I can't. I failed her."

"Not being able to save her isn't the same as failing her."

Izzy took a deep breath. "Why are we here, Brooke? Why did I have to leave my phone in the car?"

"Because I knew there were no listening devices here. I don't trust Angela not to have bugged your practice. Anything to get her precious little cause du jour a little more traction in the news." Brooke's lips twisted in a sneer as she practically spat, "She came around the house last week asking for pictures. *Pictures*. Like she has any right to pictures, after she plastered the last batch all over her damn website? I've locked her out of all my social media. She's not using my little girl to make herself famous. I won't allow it."

"Angela grieves in her own way," said Izzy quietly. "I won't argue with you over whether she'd bug my office. We both know she would. But what did you need?"

Brooke took a deep breath. "This is all...everything is broken right now. You understand that, right? You understand that everything is broken."

Izzy nodded. "I do."

"Morris's disease did something people don't know about yet."

Izzy froze. The graveyard spun around her. For a moment, it was like the floor had dropped out of the world, leaving her floating in impossible space. Finally, she found her voice and said, "That can't be possible. I would...if there had been some new discovery, I'd know about it before you would."

"Not when it's drug related and coming out of Canada. The people who've been doing this research, they're not going to start distributing their findings for another few weeks, not until they have confirmation. But one of my pharmacy school buddies works for the team that's been doing the tests, and he loved Lisa, and he dropped me a line asking me to look into a few things for him. Sent instructions and everything. I started running titers on the other technicians, and then on their kids, and then on a couple of customers. Anyone I could get the blood from. You know, checking immunity levels is just not as difficult as you medical types want to make it out to be. If you have the right equipment, it's practically a home science experiment."

Izzy didn't say anything about how it hadn't always been that way. She was too busy trying to remember how to breathe. "What did they find?"

"The damage Morris's disease does to immune memory isn't just about the memory. It's about the ability to *form* memories. Functionally, measles causes amnesia of the immune system. The body forgets all the diseases it's met before—but it can 'meet' them again. It can be *reminded*." Brooke looked at Izzy, deep sorrow and deeper determination in her eyes. "Morris's disease goes deeper. It causes something that's much closer...well, I guess closer to dementia of the limbic system. People's immune systems don't just forget. They lose the ability to learn. Either partially or completely, they lose the ability to learn. They're functionally immunocompromised for the rest of their lives."

Izzy's mouth was dry. She swallowed, hard, and asked, "Why are you telling me this?"

"Because you're a doctor and this is going to be bad, Izzy, this is going to be *so bad*." Brooke looked at her solemnly, eyes wide and anxious as a child's. She had finally, after years and years of looking, found proof that the bogeyman was real, and by God, she was going to tell the world. Or at least her sister, the one she had always been willing to depend on to make things better. The one she trusted.

"All those parents choosing to re-vaccinate their children or themselves, they're not doing anything to protect them. The herd immunity isn't coming back, because anyone who was infected with Morris's is immunocompromised now. And the people who think Morris's proved that vaccination doesn't work, they're not helping either. We can't fix this." Brooke reached into her purse and pulled out a thumb drive. "This is everything we have so far."

"Brooke. Honey. I'm just a pediatrician. I can't call the governor and tell her there's some sort of health crisis we didn't predict coming out of the Morris's outbreak. I don't have that kind of access."

"Take the drive," said Brooke. "Maybe you can't call the governor, but you can call *someone*. You'll have access to somebody that I don't, and maybe they're the one who can make some sense of this."

"If you want this spread, why did you ask me to come to a graveyard?" Izzy turned her face away. "Why not call the news? Write a blog? Do something?"

"Because it only took one person telling a big lie to kick off the entire modern anti-vaccination movement, and maybe if herd immunity hadn't already been degraded, Morris's wouldn't have been able to get a foothold," said Brooke. "I'm not going to be the next Andrew Wakefield. I'm *not*. I can't control this. All I can do is drop it and hope that someone who *can* control it will be in a position to pick it up. I'm hoping for you." She managed a weak smile. "You're my big sister. When something's wrong, I go to you and hope you can fix it. Even if you can't, it's going to come out eventually, right? So maybe we don't say anything."

Izzy's laugh was bitter. "Fix it. Because I can fix anything, right?" She reached out and touched the cool surface of Lisa's tombstone. It was rough under her fingers, real. No matter how much she wanted it, this was one nightmare she would never wake from. "I can't fix the world."

"I believe you can. No matter what, I still believe in you." Brooke set the thumb drive down next to Izzy's fingers, leaning in to kiss her cheek at the same time. "You'll do what's right with this. You'll find a way to save us."

Then she turned and walked away, leaving her sister alone in the graveyard, with proof of the end of the world waiting for her to pick it up.

"Morris's disease follows the same infectious path as the measles virus, which it appears to have mutated from either naturally or through a particularly cruel form of genetic engineering. This means that an individual with natural or acquired immunity or resistance to measles would possess that same resistance to Morris's disease. This is almost certainly why the death rates were as low as they eventually proved to be. I understand that this virus had the highest short-term fatality rate on American soil in the last century—I do want to stress 'short-term,' as there have been substantially more deaths resulting from untreated HIV, and arguably an equal number of flu deaths when looked at across a longer time span.

The true danger of Morris's disease came from and was amplified by, however unintentionally, the anti-vaccination movement. By reducing the levels of measles vaccination in the population, they reduced the resistance to measles and its derivatives—to Morris's disease. It was the reduction in vaccination rates which allowed Morris's to take hold. After that, all else became inevitable."

—from the testimony of Dr. Isabelle Gauley.

PART II: Pocket Full of Posies

3: | Incubation

1.

"DR. GAULEY, you must understand that your claims are frankly ridiculous, and verge on unreasonable fearmongering." The doctor in charge of the commission on post-Morris's disease public health glared down his nose at Izzy, every inch of him seeming to demand an apology for having the temerity to even imply that she had the right to appear before him. "Do you understand that we are in a delicate position right now? People are frightened. They don't need you making things worse."

"The data is good," she said, resisting the urge to touch her hair, to straighten her jacket. These people didn't deserve her at her best. They barely deserved her at her worst. "The Canadian commission is preparing to publish their findings. I've checked each of their tests myself, and I've been able to consistently reproduce their results. The immunocompromisation is real, and it's not going to go away because you don't want to frighten people."

"What would you suggest?" asked another of the doctors. "That we quarantine all Morris's survivors for their own protection?"

"No," said Izzy promptly. The commission looked relieved. She continued, "Their numbers are too great, and if I may be blunt, we lack the resources for that sort of undertaking. It's simply not possible. What's more, they're going to need an increasing amount of medical care over the next several years. Resources need to be devoted to eradicating Morris's disease, through whatever means necessary, including aggressive quarantine. The CDC and USAMRIID are going to have their work cut out for them here at home, and I'm expecting the World Health Organization to have its hands full for the foreseeable future. We simply don't have the *ability* to guarantee that those who have yet to be exposed will remain unexposed."

"Young lady," said the first doctor. "If you're proposing what I believe you're proposing—"

Doggedly, Izzy continued, speaking over him without hesitation. "The fact of the matter is, the only population we currently have which has not been vitally and incurably immunocompromised are those individuals, regardless of other medical conditions, who have yet to be exposed to an airborne pathogen which is still moving through the population. It hasn't burned itself out. It may never burn itself out. This is, until we find a vaccine which can *prevent* Morris's disease, and a treatment for the long-term effects on the immune system, the new normal. We're going to need blood from people who are still healthy enough to give blood. We're going to need to protect people who were born with medical conditions which have left them susceptible to infection regardless of Morris's disease—unless, of course, you'd prefer to see them all die as the immunocompromising virus spreads and their systems can't react."

"You can't be serious." The older doctor didn't sound pompous anymore. If anything, he sounded stunned.

"I'm afraid I am." Izzy looked from face to face, trying to guess how many of them would be with her. Not that it necessarily mattered. There were other ways to accomplish what needed to be done. Maybe not as easily, and certainly not as openly, but still.

"You're talking about…what, exactly?" She knew the doctor who was now leaning forward and looking at her with narrow-eyed intensity. He was a surgeon, not among the best in the country, but solid enough. His patients, for the most part, lived. He had operated on a few of her kids. "Setting up some sort of camp?"

"There's an island," she said calmly. "Tilman Island, to be specific, off the coast of Washington State. There are buildings there already, but there are currently no inhabitants, due to the wildlife refuge located there. We are requesting permission from this commission and from the governor to expand those buildings and begin occupation of the wildlife refuge. Under the circumstances, I don't think I'm alone in considering the preservation of human life to be more important than the nesting sites of some seabirds. Let them move to Long Island. It's larger, and the Willapa National Wildlife Refuge is more established. It can absorb the population."

"You want to build a biodome," said the first doctor.

Izzy nodded. "I do. Far enough from the mainland that we can still allow access to the outdoors. Children need to see the sky, and we're fortunate in that Morris's disease isn't zoonotic. We don't need to worry about it coming over with a seagull."

"How will you prevent it from coming in with parents or family members who want to visit?" demanded the second doctor. "Until there's a treatment—"

"That's exactly it," said Izzy. "Until there's a treatment, we prevent Morris's disease from making the jump off the mainland by not allowing anyone to enter. We grow our own vegetables. We sterilize everything else that comes in. We get our deliveries by drone whenever possible. I'm talking about full isolation, not of the sick, but of the healthy. It is the only way we will see them through this."

She looked from face to face before adding, in a soft voice, "Please."

In the end, the committee deliberated for an hour before returning with their verdict.

"You had to know there was no way we would allow this project to proceed," said the first doctor. "Even considering your history with the virus, this is too extreme. You would shatter families and confiscate public land in pursuit of a safety that you will never be able to achieve. I'm sorry, Dr. Gauley. But the ruling of the United States Commission for Resolution of Morris's Disease is no."

"Thank you," she said, and rose. "I understand."

By midnight that night, she would be gone.

Everything proceeded from there.

2.

"DR. GAULEY?" The practice was dark, save for a single bulb burning in the doctor's private office. Mark hesitated before reaching for the light switch. Something about chasing away these shadows seemed terribly permanent, like a step that, once taken, could not be taken back.

A door slammed behind him. He jumped and whirled, hand going to his chest as if that alone would be enough to keep his traitor heart from leaping up into his throat. Sandy emerged from the gloom, her bright pink coat rendered a chalky grey by the lack of light, clutching the strap of her purse with both hands.

"She called you too?" she asked, voice barely louder than a whisper.

"Yeah," he said. "Any idea why?"

"She's been distant lately," said Sandy. "With me, anyway. You've been working with her for longer. I thought maybe…" She trailed off and shrugged helplessly.

"I wish," said Mark. He turned back toward the office and that single burning bulb. "Doc? You here?"

"I ran blood panels on you both last week," said a voice from behind them.

Mark jumped a full foot into the air as he whirled around, somehow landing between Sandy and the voice. Sandy screamed, the sound high and shrill and terrified. It was quickly cut off when she saw Dr. Gauley standing wearily in the door to the supply room, her white lab coat very visible despite the general gloom. Everything about her looked worn to the bone. Even her hair lacked its customary curl. But her shoulders were square, and what little of her expression could be seen seemed grimly determined.

"Neither of you caught Morris's disease during the outbreak," continued Dr. Gauley. "Dayna and Lin both did, unfortunately. Neither of them was ever symptomatic, but they've got the markers. They were infected. I'd have to do more tests to determine how badly their immune systems were compromised, but some of the new research out of Canada indicates that the damage doesn't happen all at once—it's a slow erosion in individuals who never became visibly ill. Meaning the only way to know for sure who's clean is to do the tests."

"What the hell are you talking about, Doc?" Mark took a step to the side, clearing Sandy's field of vision. "You scared the crap out of us. Not cool."

"I didn't authorize any bloodwork," said Sandy nervously. "I think I would have noticed if I had. What…?"

"I needed to know if either of you had been infected. You're clean, thank God, because I'm going to need you."

"You're not making any sense, Doc," said Mark. "And can we get back to how you got our blood without asking us? Because that matters. That matters a *lot*."

"Not right now, it doesn't." Izzy looked between them and sighed before starting for her office. "Follow me. I don't have much time to explain, and you don't have much time to decide."

Obedience was a difficult habit to break, no matter how trying the circumstances. Mark and Sandy followed their employer—their friend—through the darkened practice, until she stepped into her office. The light Mark had seen from the door was her desk lamp, angled toward her laptop, so that the glare rendered the screen unreadable. Dr. Gauley kept walking until she reached the desk. There was a cardboard box on her chair. She pulled open a drawer and began calmly, systematically transferring its contents.

"Morris's disease enhances the natural immunosuppressant qualities of measles," said Dr. Gauley, without looking up. "Brooke has been feeding me data from a research group in Canada. They haven't gone public because they were afraid of starting a panic. I think it's a little late to be worried about that, don't you?"

Mark's stomach turned to ice. "You're not serious."

"Very. Unfortunately, all their data has been independently verifiable: while it's unclear how much Morris's disease causes the body to forget—it seems to vary from case to case—it absolutely causes immune amnesia, with a twist. Once infected, the immune system loses the ability to form defenses against anything it's forgotten. Someone whose body forgets how to contend with, say, the H1N1 flu due to exposure to Morris's can never build an immunity again. Not through exposure, not through vaccination, not through any known path. They're at risk again, for all of it. Now and forever, they're in danger."

"I think I'm going to be sick," said Sandy, voice muffled by the hand clasped across her mouth. "We have to...we have to..."

"What, Sandy?" Dr. Gauley finally looked up, eyes blazing in the insufficient light. "Panic the country before we've managed to establish a safe place for those who haven't yet been exposed? For the infants, and the cancer patients, and the others who won't be able to get a vaccination against Morris's even if we can create one, and who will be risking a lifetime of immunosuppression if they ever become infected? I went to the Commission. I hoped they'd be willing to fund the creation of a...a biodome of sorts, to keep the uninfected safe until an answer can be found. They said no. They said it would be unthinkable a cure, or at least a vaccination, can be found. We've got anti-abortion zealots trying to ram through mandatory vaccinations that aren't going to do any good *anyway*, we've got politicians treating Morris's disease like it's an ordinary outbreak, and we've got a tiny, tiny window where there's half a chance in hell for us to do *anything* to keep people safe, and these people—these *people*—will fritter it all away scoring points on each other. Something has to be done. We don't have much time."

"Doc...?" said Mark carefully.

"We have private investors. Not enough, God knows it could never be enough, but one of them made billions during the first dot-com boom, and he has three children with clean blood panels. One of them has been on anti-rejection drugs since she had a kidney transplant at age four." Dr. Gauley slammed a drawer with more force than strictly necessary. "He wants her to be safe. He wants her to grow up. And he's willing to devote as many resources as we need to making sure that can happen."

"'We'?" asked Sandy.

"I need you." Dr. Gauley looked between them. "I need people I know, people I can trust. People who understand what it means to work with me. You went into medicine because you wanted to help people. You wanted to save lives. This is your opportunity to put your money where your mouths are. Come with me."

"Where are you going?" asked Mark.

"I can't tell you unless you're coming," said Dr. Gauley. She smiled, regretfully. "I don't want to leave either of you behind. I was genuinely hoping we'd be able to do this through the proper channels. Now...all I can do is hope we get as far as possible before someone comes to try and shut us down. Brooke is already there, arranging for local help."

"Local help?" Mark looked at Sandy, who was still staring blankly at Dr. Gauley. "Local help with what, exactly?"

"Construction. Staffing. Sterilization and temporary housing, where relevant. We can't insist that everyone involved at this stage be clean of Morris's disease, but there are various methods of buying silence, and not all of them involve money. We're going to be testing their families, and their children. Anyone who comes up clean will be moved to the tent city that's been established near our new property. Guaranteed spots, all of them. We're not going to save the world. That's a job for someone else. But we're going to save a lot of lives, and I have colleagues who are already, quietly, talking about following our model. We get to be pioneers. I want both of you with me."

Mark hesitated for a long moment before he said, "This sounds like a lot of secrecy, Doc, which makes me suspect this isn't all going to be strictly legal, or strictly ethical. What happens if we say no, we don't want to get involved in something like this?"

"I'm not going to kill you, if that's what you're asking," said Dr. Gauley. "I wouldn't be asking you to do this if I didn't love and trust you both. So if you don't want to be a part of this endeavor, well, I'll understand, I honestly will. I'm asking a lot. And if you say 'no,' I'll ask you to stay here. Come in tomorrow morning and open the practice like nothing has happened, like you never saw me, like you have no idea where I might be. You can play innocent, and I'm certain you'll both be fine. Your records are impeccable. Any practice or hospital in this area would be lucky to have you. I mailed letters of recommendation to everyone on the staff this morning, the two of you included."

"Why, if you were going to ask us to go with you?" asked Mark.

Sandy's elbow caught him lightly just below the ribs. "Because leaving a letter for everybody means it's harder to know who she took with her, and who just took off when the doctor disappeared," she said. "It's tactical. It's smart. But she's banking a lot on the idea that we won't tell on her."

"I am," agreed Dr. Gauley. "I'm really hoping that your desire to do good is going to outweigh your desire to follow the rules. So what do you say? Will the two of you run away from home with me, so that we can try to save the world?"

Mark and Sandy exchanged a look. Sandy smiled, the expression surprisingly wicked on her normally sweet face.

"I guess we were just waiting for you to ask," she said.

3.

AIR TRAVEL, disrupted by Morris's disease and the ensuing chaos, had yet to return to pre-pandemic levels of ease or affordability. More importantly, due to the role it had played in spreading the pandemic, it had lost any pretense of anonymity. Anyone who so much as sneezed in an airport was in danger of detention until they could be given a clean bill of health. Trains, which were just as capable as airplanes of carrying disease, had slightly less effective security measures, and were hence the new preferred means of travel for people who were trying to slip under the radar—assuming people chose to travel at all.

All of this, combined, was the reason dawn found Dr. Isabelle Gauley standing on the tarmac of Buchanan Field in Concord, California, clutching an old-fashioned suitcase in one hand, her too-heavy coat flapping in the morning breeze. She kept her eyes fixed on the road running past the airfield, counting seconds and praying that when she finally saw a car, it would be the one she'd asked for, and not the police coming to take her in for questioning.

I had to go before the Commission, she thought. *I had to make sure my attempt to do the right thing was on the record.* The difference between hero and villain was so frequently in the paperwork that most people never thought to file. When this all came to light—or when it all fell apart—she was going down knowing that she had done everything she possibly could to ensure that history had her on the right side. She was a hero. Everything she had done, from the very beginning, had been about the preservation of mankind.

Everything.

Motion out of the corner of her eye drew her attention, and she turned to see the pilot hired for today's journey looking at her curiously. She held up a hand, fingers splayed, signaling for five more minutes. He nodded, curiosity fading into serene displeasure. This sort of trip was dangerous even when everything happened as intended. Changing the plan was, well…

It was just short of suicide. If they weren't here in five minutes, she'd have to leave them. She wouldn't have a choice. There was no difference between "running late" and "not coming at all" at this stage: the plane was leaving, and if they weren't on it, they weren't coming. Not now, not later. Not ever. She had trusted them once. If they couldn't live up to that trust, she couldn't offer it to them again. No matter what.

"Come on, Mark," she muttered. Mark, she had been almost sure would join her. His relationship with his parents was strained, thanks to his profession and his sexuality; they might have been able to deal with having a male nurse in the family if he hadn't also been gay. His twin brother was eight hundred miles away, and the father of two children, both of whom had managed to dodge Morris's. Once they were up and running, if the children tested negative for antigens, she had been planning to ask Mark if he wanted to bring his niece and nephew up to join them.

Not the brother, sadly. He was a station operator, helping passengers navigate the over-crowded and often confusing rail system. There was almost no possibility he'd escaped infection, even if it had never gone above the subclinical. Odds were that his immune system was still mostly intact, losing only a few small, unimportant pieces of its learned memory. He could live for a very long time, content in the knowledge that his children were safe someplace that would give them the chance to live even longer.

Parents could give up their children when it was the only way to save them. Of that, she was absolutely sure.

Sandy had always seemed like the harder sell. She was adopted, and she loved her family, but had moved to California to "find" herself when she realized that the Mormon church was not for her, while it was everything to them. She had never been able to locate her biological parents, and had given up about a year after coming to work for Izzy. She'd always said that she was looking for something more. Exactly what that meant was less than clear. The thought that breaking the rules might be a step further than she wanted to go wasn't a difficult one to have.

But oh, Izzy had been hoping at least one of them would come.

She was starting to turn away when a small blue sedan came roaring down the sleepy street at a speed that would absolutely have attracted the attention of law enforcement, had law enforcement been anywhere in the area. She stopped, her breath catching in her throat as the car screeched into the turn-off for the airfield, finally coming to a stop not fifteen feet away.

Sandy tumbled out of the driver's side, while Mark emerged more decorously, a backpack in one hand and Sandy's suitcase in the other. The suitcase was bright pink and decorated in Hello

Kitty decals. Izzy put her hands over her mouth, forcing her relieved laughter to stay inside.

"Sorry we're late, Doc," said Mark. "Somebody insisted on weighing her luggage eight times to be sure it was within the weight limits you set."

"Somebody also had to feed her fish and leave a note saying that she—that I—was going to Reno for the weekend, can you please make sure they don't starve," said Sandy primly. "My roommate will feed them, and when I don't come back, she'll point people in the wrong direction before she can point them in the right one. I thought that was worth a few minutes delay."

"It wouldn't have been if we'd missed the flight," said Mark. "Right, Doc?"

"You're both right," said Izzy, lowering her hands. "You didn't miss the flight. I waited for you. I waited." She wanted to laugh. She wanted to cry. She wanted to take off her coat before the already-sweltering California morning baked the life from her—but they weren't going to be in California long, now, were they? They were on their way. "Come on."

The pilot was a steely-eyed ex-Coast Guard officer who had gone out of his way to know as little as possible about his passengers. He was flying them eight hundred miles up the coast. He was getting paid cash for his day's work, and he was never going to see any of them again. That was what mattered.

"We're ready," said Izzy. He grunted acknowledgment and unlocked the plane.

All the restrictions imposed on commercial aviation as a means of slowing the spread of infection had naturally created a busy web of short-hop pilots carrying goods and occasionally passengers from one place to another. Most of them didn't have the licenses to transport people, but they knew who to bribe and they knew where not to land, and most of all, they knew what not to get a reputation for carrying. Very few drug smugglers worked by air, not because of any ethical stance, but because they couldn't get anyone to move their merchandise. A drug conviction meant a pulled license, wheels down, never fly again. The pilots who were still flying were willing to take virtually any risk but that.

With four of them packed into the tiny jet, the walls felt too close and the air felt stale, creating a tense, claustrophobic atmosphere. The pilot handed out noise-blocking headsets before going into his pre-flight checklist. Izzy hung hers around her neck and looked gravely at the others.

"We won't be able to talk once we're in the air, and that's a good thing," she said, making a creepy-crawly motion with one hand. "We'll land in about five hours. When we do, we'll be taken for decontamination and head for the next stage of our journey. If either of you wants to back out, this is your last opportunity to do so."

Sandy's eyes went wide. 'Bugs?' she mouthed, mimicking the hand motion.

Izzy nodded.

"We're in now, Doc," said Mark. "If we were going to back out, we would have done it before we got here."

"Good," said Izzy, and then the engine was on, and communication stopped.

The flight was surprisingly smooth, given the small size of the plane and the alarming way the engine sometimes whined, like it was rethinking its divorce from gravity. Sandy dozed. Mark pressed his face against the small window and watched California unspool below them like some sort of magic eye picture, slowly transforming from urban sprawl to farmland and finally to forest stretching as far as he could see. Izzy, compacted into her seat, hugging her pack against her chest, watched the two of them and wondered how she had possibly been fortunate enough to assemble a team like the one around her.

Together, they would be able to survive this. She had absolute faith in *that*. She glanced at her watch. Her phone, along with anything else capable of pinpointing her location, was in the drawer of her desk at the practice. It was almost ten o'clock. The staff would be gone by now, having given up waiting for the boss and taken advantage of their unexpected day off. She couldn't be sure the protestors would have done the same, looking at the clinic's darkened windows and closed doors and seeing the opportunity to take a day for themselves. She *hoped* they would. She hoped, genuinely and sincerely and to the bottom of her heart that every single one of them had packed up their things and gone off to do something else. Something less hateful, maybe. Something less cruel.

She didn't want to kill anyone. She just wanted to make sure that she and her people had a chance to get where they were going and begin what they needed to do. There was so much work ahead of them, and so little time to accomplish it in. Nothing could be allowed to slow them down.

Nothing.

At ten o'clock precisely the incendiary device Isabelle Gauley had purchased on the Oakland black market and planted in her desk drawer exploded, destroying her office instantly, and triggering the three additional devices planted in the exam and waiting rooms. The entire structure came down with a swift, brutal elegance, burying the practice and everything it contained under the rubble. Although she would not know it for quite some time, her prayers were at least partially answered: no one was in the building when it exploded, and no one was close enough on the sidewalk outside to be hurt by the flying debris. She was not, in this case, directly responsible for any deaths.

Eleven regular protestors would be arrested for bombing the clinic. Eight of them would be detained in a local correctional facility, where one would die of a heart attack waiting for trial and another would contract—ironically enough—whooping cough from another inmate. Had his immune system not already been weakened by Morris's disease, he might have recovered. As it was, his body was burned despite the wishes of his family, part of a program intended to reduce the risk of infection.

But all that would come later. In the moment when the clinic burned, Isabelle, Mark, and Sandy were flying away, one of them hoping for the best possible outcome of a terrorist act while the others sat in quiet, almost peaceful ignorance, looking toward the future while behind them, the past burned to ashes.

4.

THE PLANE set down with a shudder and a thump, gliding to the end of the barely marked, intentionally unnamed runway and going still. The captain, flicking off the final switches to deactivate the engine, twisted in his seat.

"Out," he said brusquely. "This is as far as I go."

Without the engine's roar, the silence of the plane felt deafening. Izzy uncurled and climbed out of the cabin, leaving the others to follow her. As soon as the last of them—Mark—was on the ground, the door slammed shut, and they were alone.

"He won't come out to refuel until you're gone," said a cheerful female voice. All three turned.

The woman standing at the edge of the runway looked harmless, like a kindergarten teacher in search of a school. Her long brown hair fell in perfect soup can ringlets, framing a heart-shaped face whose dark, twinkling eyes promised finger-paints and cookies at snack time. She was wearing a sensible wool skirt over leggings, sensible brown hiking boots, and a clearly hand-knit green sweater with frayed cuffs, like it had been worn over and over again until it had become an extension of her body.

"None of the pilots who transport people like to hang around with their passengers," she continued. "As they don't know who you are or where you're going from here, the potential for them to be the source of a leak is reduced, and thus the chances of someone coming for them with a silencer and a grudge if you get caught goes way, way down. I'm Ami, I'm going to be taking you to the boat."

"Hi, Ami," said Izzy. "I'm Dr. Isabelle—"

"I know who you are," said Ami. "I've seen your files. Please, come with me." She turned and walked away from the runway, into the brush on the other side.

Izzy didn't hesitate before shrugging into her backpack, grasping the handle of her suitcase—the largest among the three of them, almost large enough to contain a body—and following. Mark and Sandy trailed along behind. The tall grasses at the runway's edge parted easily to admit them, and they were gone.

When he was interviewed by the Presidential commission investigating Isabelle Gauley's actions later—much, much later—their pilot would be able to honestly say that he didn't know where they had been heading, or even which direction they had chosen. All he knew was that he had been paid to transport three passengers to Oregon, and that the compensation had been worth the risk. Whether he still felt that way after everything that followed was almost irrelevant. It was finished, it was done, and no amount of regretting could change the past.

Ami moved through the brush with the delicacy of a dancer, never snagging her skirt on reaching branches, never stumbling or losing her balance. Sandy, the veteran of Mommy-and-Me ballet classes and solo gymnastics lessons all through her childhood, fared almost as well. She stepped around the worst obstacles and went over the rest of them, breathing easily, ankles remaining elegantly unturned. Mark and Isabelle weren't so lucky. If there was something to trip over, they tripped over it; if there was something to step on, or in, their feet found it without even trying.

By the time they emerged onto the flat, pebbly surface of the beach, Isabelle had what looked like half a hedge in her hair, and Mark looked frustrated enough to cry. They both relaxed at the sight of the sea.

"They can't expect us to walk on water," said Mark. "Right, Doc? You didn't arrange for paddle-boats or something?"

"I didn't arrange for any of this," said Izzy. "I made the first calls, but Brooke's the one who's been working with our benefactor, and he made our travel arrangements from this point onward. Don't worry. My sister wouldn't set us up to be dumped in the middle of the Pacific Ocean."

"I like how you assume that's what I'd be worried about," said Mark sourly. "That specific thing. Because wow, now that you've put that into my head, it's going to stay there. No getting rid of it from here. You're the best, Doc."

"This way," said Ami, a look of faint amusement on her face.

She led the trio down the beach to a thick copse of pine trees, their branches reaching toward the sky like silent sentinels. Pushing into the green, she left them little choice but to follow.

The trees, while thick, weren't deep; in only a few steps, they had emerged onto another, smaller slice of beach, this one obscured from all easy lines of sight. There was a boat anchored there, an inflatable with rigid boning that kept it from being overly buffeted by the waves. Ami hauled her skirt up and tucked the hem into the waistband, revealing thick legs protected by warm gray leggings.

"It's about an hour from here to where the main ship is anchored," she said. "We have space for all your luggage—this little baby has roughly the same carrying capacity as the bird you were just in. And once you're on the big fish, of course, your luggage won't even be a drop in the bucket. If anyone needs to pee, now's the time."

"There's a bathroom here?" asked Sandy eagerly.

Ami looked at her with amusement. "There's a forest," she said.

"Oh." Sandy deflated. "I can hold it for another hour."

"Suit yourself," said Ami. "All aboard who's coming aboard."

Mark glanced at Isabelle, who nodded marginally. It was too late for turning back, had been too late since the airfield. By now, the practice would be so much rubble, the fires hopefully long since extinguished, the authorities picking through the wreckage searching for the bodies they would—please, God—never find. Mark didn't know that, of course. Izzy hoped she'd be able to keep it from him, from both of them, for as long as possible. Some forms of innocence could never be recovered, only preserved.

The little boat dipped deeper into the water under their combined weight, but when Ami started the engine, it moved smoothly and without resistance, ploughing through the waves, moving them steadily away from the shore. Sandy clung to the edge, exclaiming and pointing. Mark was more taciturn, settling next to Ami at the throttle and watching the world go by. Once again, Izzy closed her eyes, sinking into the motion, hugging her bag against her chest like she thought there was some comfort in its contents.

Almost there, Lisa, she thought. Time might eventually blunt her memory of her niece, of the little girl with the trusting eyes and busy hands who had been the brightest star on her horizon for so long. Lisa was the one who'd made her really want to change the world. Lisa was the one who'd made her see that changing the world was *possible*—Lisa and, ironically, Angela, whose willingness to give her child up had changed so many worlds, all at the same time. A single person could transform everything. She had started off doing everything she did for Lisa's sake, and now, with Lisa gone, she was still doing it all for the little girl who had loved her, and trusted her, and died under her care.

We're almost there.

The sea was calm and Ami, whatever else she might be, was an excellent sailor. She steered them across the small swells and out into open water without hesitation, her hand on the tiller, her eyes on the horizon. The engine's soft whine was nothing compared to the plane three of them had been packed into so very recently; it was almost peaceful, relaxing into the moment, into the lull between difficult stages.

When the "big ship" appeared, it was small, distant, almost unbelievable as anything other than a mirage. Ami steered them closer, and bit by bit it resolved into the sort of luxury yacht available only to the extravagantly rich, the kind of people who didn't have to care about fuel costs or taxes.

Mark inched down the length of their boat toward Izzy. "Doc? You asleep?"

"Yes," she said mildly, not opening her eyes.

"This billionaire. You weren't exaggerating, were you? We're talking about billionaire here. As in, billions of dollars. So many dollars that it isn't even a thing to send a boat that looks like it belongs on TV to pick us up."

"It's probably a ship, not a boat, but yes." She kept her eyes closed. Once she opened them, this would all begin again. She wasn't quite ready for that. "Billionaire. You may have heard of him. Christopher Holland?"

"Holland?" Mark's voice broke in a brief, high squeak. "As in Holland Computing, as in the people who made my phone? Canada's answer to Steve Jobs? *That* Christopher Holland?"

"That Christopher Holland," said Izzy. "He's very concerned about his children. Which works in our favor, since his concern translates directly into funding for what we're hoping to accomplish. We found a patron with functionally bottomless pockets. Enjoy it, embrace it, and let yourself get to work."

"Speaking of getting to work, we're here," said Ami. "Dr. Gauley?"

Reluctantly, Izzy sat up, turned, and opened her eyes.

The yacht was close enough now to dominate the entire horizon. A dangling array of hooks and straps was clearly intended to lift their little boat up to deck level, where they'd be able to transfer from one vessel to the other. Izzy reached up and ran a hand through her hair, trying to force it into some semblance of decency.

"All right, everyone," she said. "This is where you start earning your paychecks."

"Not me," said Ami. "I don't work for you."

Izzy flashed her a swift, tight smile. "I think you'll find that starting now, everyone works for me."

Ami looked dubious. The hooks connected with the sockets at the sides of their boat, and it began rising slowly upward, lifted by the winches on the deck. Izzy ran her hands through her hair again. When the boat slowed and finally stopped, she was the first to her feet, stepping onto the deck of the yacht and extending her hand toward the tall, formally dressed black man who was waiting for her there.

"Mr. Holland," she said. "It's an honor to finally meet you, sir."

"Dr. Gauley," he replied. He took her extended hand in his and shook twice, firmly, before letting go. "Thank you so much for coming."

There were so many things she could have said. She could have pointed out that this, all of this, had been her idea; that her sister, working tirelessly in the memory of the daughter neither of them had been in a position to save, had been the one to realize that he might be ripe for recruitment and bring him over to their way of seeing things. She could have reminded him that without her, their glorified summer camp would have had no way of guaranteeing the medical standards they were hoping to achieve. She did none of those things.

Instead, she smiled, and said, "It's my pleasure. I'm sure we're going to do excellent things together." She waved to indicate Mark and Sandy, now stepping off the boat. "My team were kind enough to join me, which is going to make this much easier. It's always best when you don't have to bring people up to speed. I assume we're heading for the site? Are we prepared to break ground?"

Mr. Holland laughed. Izzy blinked.

"I beg your pardon?" she said. "Have I said something wrong?"

"We're not prepared to break ground," he replied. "We've done it. Almost a week ago, following your specifications. I think you'll be pleasantly surprised to find what happens when money is no longer an object. Ami?"

"Sir?"

"Notify the captain that we're ready to sail for the island. He has the coordinates."

"Sir," repeated Ami. She took off down the deck, un-hiking her skirt as she went, until it fell to swirl around her ankles once again.

Mr. Holland watched her go and chuckled indulgently. "She was Canadian Special Ops when I found her," he said. "Looking for a career change that came with steady hours, sound-proofed rooms, and the ability to eat bread again. It's amazing what a military diet for fifteen years will do to the mind's response to carbohydrates. They're practically a narcotic to her."

"Are you saying she knows how to kill a man?" asked Mark.

"I'm saying she knows twenty-seven ways to kill a man, and some of them won't leave a mark behind," said Mr. Holland. "Ami will be organizing our security teams for the site. I hope you don't consider this too forward, Dr. Gauley, but I've taken the liberty of allowing her to update the plans your sister drew out. Ms. Morris has a keen mind, but she's no tactician."

"I don't consider that anything more than utterly reasonable," said Izzy. "Brooke and I will be handling the medical and logistical sides of the facility. We're going to need experts for the other areas. Some can be hired. Others should be obligated to the facility."

For a moment—only a moment—Holland's air of general affability flickered. "As I am going to be," he said.

"Yes." It felt strange to be discussing this in the open air. They were far enough from shore that no microphone was going to record their conversation, no camera was going to capture their images, but that didn't matter. This had been the secret project for months, never revealed to anyone outside of a very small, very select group—so small and so select that it hadn't even included the two loyal staffers who now stood behind her, waiting for this to all start making sense. It had been nice to have a secret that didn't hurt to carry. She wasn't sure she'd ever have another like it. "You were approached because that obligation seemed likely to bind you to the work. You must understand, as a father, why it's important that everyone feel the way you do. That everyone be willing to die to preserve the sanctity of our walls."

"Once they're finished," he said, with some small amusement.

"Yes. Once they're finished."

"We're going to go down in history. One way or another, we're going to be remembered as the ones who built this."

"Yes." If there was any mercy in the world, his name would appear in front of hers for the rest of human history. Whether their work was referred to as Holland's vision or Holland's folly, let her be forgotten. Let her contribution to the situation be measured in survivors, and not in graves. "I suppose we are."

5.

THEY STAYED close enough to the coast to play peekaboo with the trees. The hours melted into night, until everyone retreated to their cabins to sleep. Mark passed out cold, face down on the pillow, and dreamt of saving the world. Sandy slept fitfully, waking around midnight to pray—a habit she'd almost broken—before closing her eyes again.

Izzy checked her notes, and when that was done, she checked them again, and when that was done she checked them for the third time, watching the way the data clicked together like the vertebrae of a healthy spine, each piece leading inevitably and inexorably to the next. When she realized that she was midway through the fourth review and couldn't remember anything since the end of the third, she closed her laptop and finally slept.

She woke to the awareness that the ship had stopped moving. Rising quickly, she pulled on a sweater, stepped into her shoes, and made her way to the deck. Sandy, who had always been an early riser, was already there, hands gripping the rail, eyes fixed on the island in front of them. Izzy stepped up beside her, too busy staring to say a word.

The Canadian coast was the perfect backdrop to make the scene in front of them unbelievably strange. Pristine evergreens stretched as far as the eye could see, turned into a surreal painting by distance and the sheer amount of construction equipment currently packed onto an island no more than six miles long and two miles across. A ferry port had already taken form; a crew was painting it in shades of olive and brown, making it harder to spot from a distance. Another crew was laying down the concrete to anchor the fence posts. The island they'd settled on wasn't a wildlife preserve—not like the American island she had originally tried to obtain—but there were still migratory seabirds that came here to roost, and it had been decided that it would benefit the island's eventual inhabitants if they could enjoy the beauty of the natural world while in their open-ended isolation.

Buildings were taking shape all across the island, a small community springing up where none had previously existed. It wasn't beautiful, not yet: it was too busy becoming functional to waste time on beauty. But Izzy could look at the bones of their community-to-be and see where the beauty would go, see the spaces being left open for small parks, see the places where the structures had been left that tiny bit more open than they needed to be for the sake of fitting some pleasing flourish or enhancement into the gaps.

"It's all real," breathed Sandy, casting a sidelong glance at Izzy. "Everything you said is real. We're doing this. We're actually doing this."

"We are," Izzy confirmed. Her eyes never left the island. "We can't take enough to be anything more than a stop-gap measure, but we can save a lot of lives while we're fighting the fires." She had hopes, as yet unvoiced, that this would be only the first community of its kind: that eventually there might be a string of islands stretching the length of the coast, isolating not the sick, but the healthy. Giving them the chance to stay that way, while also isolating those for whom any additional illness would be a death sentence.

"People aren't going to understand."

"People never do."

Sandy glanced at her again, a little more nervously. "We're going to require vaccination before people can come here, right? It's going to be mandatory?"

"Assuming a person *can* be vaccinated, yes, it's going to be mandatory. Maybe as much as twenty percent of our starting population will be people who have not been infected with Morris's disease, but whose immune systems aren't strong enough for vaccination against other diseases. We need to maintain herd immunity against those diseases in order to protect our population from any accidental exposure in the future."

"How is that different from what your sister's group wanted to do?"

Izzy paused. She had been anticipating this question. A lot of people were going to ask it. Governments, health organizations, reporters—both the ones who understood why she was doing this and the ones who wanted to paint her island as some sort of ark for the extremely wealthy, rather than recognizing that the people like Mr. Holland, the ones who bought their way in, were the only reason a place like this could exist at all. Walt Disney gave his children free passes to his park. Christopher Holland gave his children free passes to something a little less exciting, but a lot more likely to keep them alive.

"Angela's group is...very focused," she said carefully. "They want universal vaccination now, and they want it regardless of what it costs. There are ways to make vaccination mandatory as a matter of societal benefit, without infringing on any other rights of the individual—no one was exempt from the smallpox campaigns, because the societal benefit outweighed the personal loss. And no one wants to mandate vaccination for people who are willing to commit to living in purposefully isolated societies, for example, even though that can mean preserving viruses that might otherwise be extinguished. But Angela wants universal vaccination badly enough that she's partnered with people who want to use that as a doorway to doing away with bodily autonomy."

"Yes," said Sandy. "I mean...I understand why we need the right to make decisions about our own bodies, but my family...I don't think I could ever get an abortion. It would feel too much like killing a baby. If we're insisting that parents vaccinate their children so that they don't die, how is that any different?"

Izzy caught her breath and counted carefully to ten. She'd always known that Sandy came from a more conservative background than most of the staff. She loved and trusted her anyway. The woman was smart, compassionate, well-trained, and willing to do whatever was necessary to take care of the children who needed her. If she couldn't convince Sandy of the reasons behind her choices…

They would still be her choices. She would make them, and she would stand by them, and when the time came, if necessary, she would die to defend them. But the world would paint her as a villain much sooner, and with much less reason.

"People are going to keep arguing about abortion rights until we have the capability to fully incubate a human zygote outside the body, without involving use of anyone else's organs, and then I'm sure the argument will turn to whether someone has the right to bring a child with your DNA into the world without your consent," said Izzy. "It's not just about morality. It never has been. It's about control, and the privileging of a potential life above an existing one. I believe, firmly, that I should get to make choices about my body insofar as they impact *me*. I don't want to be pregnant, and if I ever became pregnant, despite my best efforts, I would end it. I would do so long before any rational person could say that I was terminating a human life, and I wouldn't feel bad about it. That's me. Your choice might be different, but it still needs to be *your* choice, and because you're making it before that zygote has the potential to exist outside your body, no one else should be involved.

"For all that my sister's organization is happy to paint it as the same, vaccination isn't about you. It's about being a part of a society. Yes, it's your body, and no, the argument that forced

vaccination is a violation of bodily autonomy isn't entirely spe-
cious, but the insistence on putting it on a level with abortion
rights is ridiculous. We have quarantine. Quarantine says that the
government can impede your ordinary movement if you present
a danger to others. Vaccination should be treated as something
on the same level. You get vaccinated, not because you want to
protect yourself, but because you want to be a part of society, and
being a part of society means protecting everyone around you."

Sandy frowned. "I don't understand how that makes us
different."

"We're not making laws. We're not saying 'this is how we
legislate away your bodily autonomy.' We're making rules for a
private facility, run independently of the government. If those
rules include mandatory vaccination for everyone without a medical reason why that isn't an option, we're well within our rights.
We're not hiding anything."

That was a lie. They were hiding so very, very many things,
some of which Sandy would never—if Izzy was clever and continued to do things according to her carefully designed plan—know
about. But it was close enough to the truth to count, and hopefully that would see them through the next several stages of this
plan, until they could shut the doors and know that everything
was as it had to be.

Footsteps on the deck behind them stopped Sandy from
asking her next question. They both turned to see Christopher
Holland approaching with Mark trailing along behind him, the
latter still wiping the sleep out of his eyes.

"Good morning," said Mr. Holland. He waved a hand to indicate the island, his eyes on Izzy. "Do you like it? Is it everything
that you hoped it would be?"

"I'm going to need to see the layouts for each building, and the specifications for the medical facilities, but at first glance... yes." Izzy couldn't resist stealing another glance at the island, where piece by piece, her dream for the salvation of humanity was becoming something real.

"Yes," she said. "It really is."

4: | Latency

1.

MONEY, IT seemed, was the axis on which the entire world turned. The delays Izzy was accustomed to experiencing went away when a check with an infinite number of zeroes was waved in front of the contractors and specialists responsible for bringing her dream to life. There were still breaks in the process—no amount of money would make concrete set faster, make paint dry before it was ready, or remove a large, invasive swarm of bees from the air vents, although it was money that brought the beekeepers with their swarm removal tools and their clever bee-safe vacuum. On the whole, however, everything progressed faster and more smoothly than she ever could have hoped.

Mark and Sandy found places for themselves with the teams responsible for stocking and outfitting the medical facilities, asking questions and coming up with list after list of necessary supplies that had somehow been missed or overlooked by the people doing the initial ordering. Brooke's pharmacy was almost ready to open for business, such as it was, but the clinics all needed additional material. Staffing was being handled by Mr. Holland, who had promised her two surgeons and a general practitioner by the end of the month. They were going to need an optometrist, dentists, and a dozen other medical professionals, but those positions could wait to be filled until after they had accomplished the first, and most important stages of construction.

"Big day today," said Brooke, stepping up next to Izzy. A boatload of contractors was leaving, heading back to the mainland, where their hefty paychecks and non-disclosure agreements would hopefully keep them quiet for a little longer. "What are you going to do during decontamination?"

"I have some research to finish, and my quarters were sterilized yesterday," said Izzy. "You?"

"Going to read a book. We're still allowed to have lives, Izzy. Everything doesn't have to be about what we're building here." Brooke laughed a little, bitterly. "If I were Angela, I'd say you were trying to out-grieve me."

"We both know that isn't true. Everyone processes sorrow in their own way and at their own speed. We'll be grieving in our own ways for years, and neither of us is letting Lisa down by doing it."

Brooke put a hand on her shoulder and squeezed. "You don't have to solve the world's problems all by yourself, Izzy. You're allowed to stop and breathe, and remember that you're alive. We're going to change things, you and me. We're going to give these children a place where they can grow up safely. Isn't that enough reason to give yourself a break?"

"I don't think I remember how."

Brooke sighed. "I wish you'd try."

Izzy turned to offer her sister a wan smile. "With everything that's happened to you, with everything that's *still* happening out there, how can you be so hopeful?" Canada was trying to thread the needle, separating the question of mandatory vaccination from the issue of bodily autonomy. Even if they succeeded—and she believed they would; the matter was too urgent, and the first potential vaccines for Morris's disease were rolling off the assembly lines, useful only if people actually *used* them—it wouldn't help them as much as they needed it to. Herd immunity required everyone be willing to put the health of the community first. Unless Canada was willing to close the borders, the proximity of America and its vast, unvaccinated population was going to keep chipping away at herd immunity, and the outbreaks would continue.

The outbreaks would always continue. As long as there were people to infect, the outbreaks would continue.

"Because my sister is the smartest person I know, and she's finding solutions." Brooke matched Izzy's smile with a much brighter smile of her own. "You may not be some fancy virologist with a magic lab that can solve everything before the end of the episode, but you're still coming up with ways to make things better. You're going to save as much of the world as you can, and I'm going to be right here with you while it happens. I'm going to know that Lisa is resting easy, because you did the right thing every time you had the opportunity."

"I don't deserve you," said Izzy.

"Nope." This time, Brooke's smile was bright and wicked. "No one really does, don't you think? But you got me anyway, so you'd better enjoy it as long as that filing error is controlling the universe. Now if you'll excuse me, I need to go make sure my pharmacy is properly locked down before the sterilization protocols begin."

She walked away. Izzy watched her go before turning, with a sigh, back to the dock. Another ferry was leaving. Another load of people who knew this place existed, but would never set foot on the island again. Another security risk.

They had…so many things already in place, and so many more were coming, medications and medical supplies and food and electronics. All the sorts of things that someone with more greed than ethical sense might look at and see as an easy score. After all, they were just a bunch of scientists and medical nerds setting up some sort of elaborate summer camp in the middle of nowhere; easy enough to swoop in and take what wasn't guarded.

She hoped, to the bottom of her soul, that none of them would try to take what looked so easy to have. The island's security system was so much more robust, and so much more lethal, than anyone not involved in its creation understood. Honestly, she wasn't even sure *she* understood it. Ami had been overseeing the installation and staffing, and apart from reviewing a few blood tests to be sure that all of their prospective live-in officers were suited to the island's requirements, Izzy had stayed safely out of reach. This was her space, her sanctuary, but she wasn't fool enough to think that she could become an expert in absolutely every aspect of its maintenance.

Morris's disease, like the measles, could be transmitted through fomite contact—tiny particles of viral matter clinging to walls or furnishings. With the last of the compromised crews leaving the island by noon, the remaining workers would be going through and sterilizing every inch of the constructed environment. The wild areas, the beaches and the forests, would remain off-limits for the next three years, giving the virus, if it was present at all, the time to die naturally. No one would ever be infected here. No one would breach the wall.

"Doc?"

Izzy turned. Mark was behind her, holding up his bare wrist as if to show her the watch he wasn't wearing.

"It's time," he said. "Sandy asked me to come and make sure you got to cover before the clouds rolled in."

"Thank you," said Izzy, with an earnest smile. She followed him away from the rail, through the staff door that would take them to the underground tunnels and hence to their respective living quarters. Mark and Sandy had been good choices. Oh, they'd been upset when they heard about the destruction of the clinic, but they had yet to outright accuse her of orchestrating it. She supposed it must be difficult for them to convince themselves that someone like her would willingly destroy something she had spent that much time and effort building, even if she had never been intending to return.

An hour later, she was curled in the corner of her bed with her laptop open on her knees, running another simulation against the most recent Morris's data sets. There was a boom from outside her steel-shuttered window. She looked up, and smiled as it was followed by two more, both of them slightly farther away. The decontamination protocol was running properly. They would be ready to open on time.

Everything was going according to plan.

2.

"MR. HOLLAND, please, sit down." Izzy closed her laptop and moved it to one side, smiling her best, most professional smile at the man who had been responsible for building everything around her. "Sandy just called to let me know that your children's latest blood panels have come up as expected. We'll be ready to make the transfer this afternoon. We'll get them settled, and then begin the screening of our next wave of candidates. You understand that the comfort of your children is our first focus, to be followed by so much more."

"Yes," he said brusquely, sinking into the offered seat and eyeing her warily. "None of this is new. Why am I here, exactly?"

"Sandy also informs me that your daughter was talking about a trip to Nova Scotia to see her grandparents. I wanted to ask you myself whether this was childish enthusiasm, or whether you'd been making promises you will be unable to keep."

Mr. Holland frowned. "My mother loves her grandchildren."

"Enough to kill them?"

His eyes widened. "Excuse me?"

"We're establishing a sterile environment for a reason, Mr. Holland. We're trying to guarantee that individuals not yet exposed to Morris's disease and its devastating after-effects will never have to deal with the consequences of the virus. Once a resident of the island is checked in, this is where they need to remain until a full and comprehensive treatment has not only been developed, but tested and distributed on a global scale. Vaccinating Canada does nothing for America. Vaccinating America does nothing for Mexico. This is another smallpox situation: we must, for the sake of humanity, come together and eradicate this scourge. As I don't see that happening within the next few weeks, I have to ask, again, does your mother love your children enough to kill them?"

Mr. Holland bristled. "I paid for this place. I should receive special considerations."

"I was afraid you'd say that, even before I knew who 'you' were; I predicted this outcome when I sent Brooke into the world to look for funding for the impossible." Izzy calmly plucked a piece of paper from the pile on her desk and held it out toward Mr. Holland. "You signed this."

He took the paper, looking at it as if he had never seen it before, even though it was his signature at the bottom, even though he recognized, in a vague way, the text of the first few paragraphs. He had skimmed it initially, signing it along with a dozen other papers, construction contracts and staffing agreements and investment commitments. This time he read more carefully. Halfway down the sheet he stopped, paling, and looked up.

"You can't do this," he said.

"You're right," said Izzy. "You're also wrong. I can absolutely do this. Ami has full control of the island's security—and while I honestly think she'd be loyal to you in any other circumstances, do you know she has two little sisters? Eleven and nine, respectively. They were never sick. Their blood panels came back clean, and they're currently in the isolation camp, waiting for the island to open. She's saving them. She can only do that if this place remains as clean as we promised it was going to be. So in this one case, under this one set of pressures, I think she'll side against you to protect them."

She leaned forward, looking at him with an implacable, terrifying calm. Mr. Holland moved involuntarily back in his chair.

"You can, of course, pull your funding from this facility. It's your money, although contractually, we won't be liable for anything already spent—you made your donations and investments of your own free will—and you could close our doors if you wanted to. You could try again. Find another island, one you haven't already deeded to a group of medical professionals who didn't want to play nicely when you decided the rules didn't apply to you. Take your children out of their sterile environment at will. When they get sick, when they lose their ability to fight off other diseases, you can tell them it was worth it if it meant they got to see their grandmother a few additional times before they died."

Mr. Holland stared at her. Finally, in a subdued tone, he said, "You're a monster."

"I know exactly what I am," said Izzy calmly. "I've never pretended to be anything else. I'm here because you wanted a way to protect your children from what's coming. For all my faults, for all my monstrosity, I acknowledge what I am. If you want me to do my job, please, allow me to do it. If you would rather pretend the world hasn't changed, you're free to do so. I hope you understand that you'll be killing your children by loving them."

"A monster," Mr. Holland repeated.

"May I assume you won't be removing your children from the isolation facility?"

He looked away. "I'll tell my mother they can't come to visit just yet. Maybe next year."

"If we can find a vaccine for the uninfected and a treatment for the survivors, it's possible." It wasn't likely. Vaccination wasn't the only issue with Morris's disease. Those who had already been infected and survived couldn't be vaccinated via normal means— not before a treatment for the immune system crash had been found.

None of that was going to come from the island. Teams of medical researchers around the world were trying to pull Morris's disease apart and find a way to render it less of a threat to the human race. Biotech labs with large staffs and better equipment and budgets that a single eager billionaire could never hope to match were attacking the problem. The island had a pediatrician, two nurses, a pharmacist, and an incoming medical staff aimed at keeping their residents healthy and happy, not at working medical miracles.

The cure, the treatment, when they were found—if they were found—would be found elsewhere. The island would do something equally vital, and in some ways far more essential.

The island would make sure there were people left to treat.

Not enough. A single facility could never have contained enough people to continue a human culture, much less the entire species. But where there was one, there could be more, and where there were more, there would be hope. As long as they instituted and followed strict isolation protocols, they could keep Morris's disease at bay long enough for that solution to be found. A few missed vacations would be a small price to pay.

Mr. Holland rose, looking subtly older than he had when he first entered. "I knew what I was signing when I signed these contracts," he said, letting the piece of paper drift back to her desk. "I knew the choices I was making were for the benefit of my children, now, and my family name, later. But I never thought about what it was going to mean for their *lives*."

"We never think about what our choices are going to mean for the lives of the ones we love," said Izzy. "We only think about what they're going to mean for us. If we're lucky, we're not the only ones who have to live with them."

"When has a choice of yours ever ruined anyone's life?"

Izzy stood. Her legs were shaking but her back was straight, and when she looked at Mr. Holland it was with the cold, clear gaze of someone who had long since run out of things to lose.

"We're done here," she said. "Thank you for being willing to discuss this matter with me. I am genuinely sorry if things didn't turn out the way you wanted them to."

Then she turned, before he could say another word, and walked away.

3.

THE ISLAND opened to residents, officially, on a Wednesday afternoon. The first boat from the isolation facility contained, among others, Ami Locklear's two younger sisters, and all three of the Holland children. The eldest, Chris Jr., stood at the rail, staring wide-eyed and solemn at the approaching island. The youngest, Michael, sat with his sister while she read to him from a brightly-colored children's book, and neither of them looked up once, as if they already knew more than they ever cared to about their destination.

Sandy stood next to Mark on the dock, a fixed smile on her face that almost compensated for the way her hands were clenched together behind her back, knuckles gone white from the pressure. "Are we doing the right thing?" she asked, voice pitched low. She didn't need to bother: the roar of the incoming ferry's engine was loud enough that no one could have heard her.

The route was preprogrammed, completely controlled by autonomous systems. There *was* a ferry captain, a sweet older man named Albert whose blood panels had come back clean the day before he'd been hired. He was going to be sharing an apartment with his husband and two grandchildren. In order to maintain his position on the island's staff, he had already entered the voluntary quarantine that would keep him from ever contacting another outsider. Any adjustments he made to the ferry's path would be done from the sealed control room, and would hopefully be necessary only in emergency situations. His job was considered a dangerous one, with the potential to bring him into contact with outsiders: his contract, consequentially, included housing and care for his family even if he became infected and had to be returned to the world outside the island.

"It's going to be fine," said Mark. "Everyone on the ferry is coming because they want to." Or because their parents wanted them to, or their guardians, or someone else with the power to exile them to a tiny island on the edge of the Pacific, far away from anything they knew or understood. This was going to be their home for the next...well, forever, maybe. The children would grow up here, go to school here—both in the tiny schoolhouse and over the internet—and if all went well, one day leave for a world where they didn't need to worry about Morris's disease or all the secondary infections it so blithely invited to the party. But that day, if it was ever going to come, was a very, very long time in the future. Right now, this was a summer camp with no end date.

"These ones are," said Sandy. "What about the next ones? Or the ones after them? You know we're not going to be all-volunteer forever."

"I know," said Mark. He was quiet for a moment, watching the ferry come closer. Finally, abruptly, he said, "It's like we're acting out the Pied Piper, only we wound up on the wrong side of the story."

Sandy only nodded.

"Maybe someday we'll be a fairy tale. Wouldn't that be a kick and a half? 'The Kingdom of Needles' or something. The place where children disappear to live out the plague."

"Not the only place," said Sandy, and then the ferry was pulling up snug with the dock, and there was no more time for conversation, only for stepping forward, all professional smiles, and greeting their new citizens.

The children had been divided before landing, as had the adults; each group had as close to an equal mix of the two as possible without separating family groups. Ami was already on the island. Sandy saw her approaching Mark's group as they made their way down the path toward the apartments, saw the strangely terrifying woman, who could make a floral sundress look like full plate armor, drop to her knees and open her arms for her shrieking, laughing sisters. The other children came with the guardians who would be living with them here on the island, or, as in the case of Christopher Holland's children, came alone.

Those three children were looking at her now, Chris Jr. warily, Michael and Serene with bright eyes and curious gazes. This still seemed like a holiday to them, an exciting adventure that would end soon enough, but would be entertaining until it did.

"Hello," she said brightly, clapping her hands together. "My name is Sandy, and I'm going to be your tour guide today. Tomorrow, I'll be one of your medical intake supervisors. Now, I know you were told what that means during your shipboard orientation. Can any of you explain it to me?"

Michael put up his hand. Sandy pointed to him.

"It means you're going to take more blood and compare it to the blood you already took, and ask us a bunch of questions we've already answered, and I don't know *why*," he said. "Can you tell us *why*?"

A general murmur ran through the children and adults alike. It held no edge of mutiny, only confusion, but she had worked enough with groups back when she was still volunteering at the Temple in Salt Lake City to know how quickly curiosity could turn into open rebellion.

Oh, Dr. Gauley, she thought helplessly. *You need to be so much more careful than you think you do.*

"For the duration of your stay here on the island, we're going to be your primary source of medical care," said Sandy. "Almost everything you need, from asthma inhalers to dental surgery, can happen right here. It's our goal to make sure that no one ever *has* to leave. And that means that it's important for us to get to know you both mentally and physically. By running those tests ourselves, even if someone else has already run them, we'll be able to know that we have the best, most up-to-date information. And we'll have cookies after you give blood, so it's really a pretty good deal."

About half the group laughed. Chris Jr. didn't.

"How long are you going to keep us here?" he demanded.

Sandy managed, barely, to conceal her wince. This was the question she and Mark had both been dreading. She hoped he'd managed to put it off a little longer than she had, while at the same time hoping petulantly that he was dealing with just as much crap as she was.

"Until the danger passes," she said. "Your father sent you to live with us because it's safe here, and he wants you to be protected."

"Safe and *boring*," he muttered.

It was sometimes easy for adults to think of children as objects, things that could be moved around on a whim. Sandy had been a pediatric nurse for too long to fall into that comfortable delusion. Children were people from the moment they came into the world, and like all people, they had their own ideas about things. They *wanted*. Serene was here because she had to be: leaving her in the world with Morris's disease wiping out immune protections would have been certain death for her, and for the children like her, many of whom were currently on their way to this very island. Chris Jr. and Michael, on the other hand, could have stayed at home and taken their chances with the rest of the world.

They probably had friends. Maybe even the kind of friends who liked to hold hands and trade kisses when there were no parents watching. They had favorite places and favorite foods and so many favorite things that couldn't be packed onto a small ferry and sent to an island in the middle of nowhere. Sandy was willing to bet that none of the kids standing in front of her had been asked if they *wanted* to go, not even the ones whose parents were standing beside them.

It wasn't hard to conjure a sympathetic smile and say, "It's probably going to be a little boring in the beginning, yeah. We're still figuring things out, and we have a lot of work to do. But I bet you can find something here that would be worse without you, and tell us how to make it better. This is our home now. If we all pitch in, it's going to be a good one. Now, if you'll all follow me…"

Sandy started walking. The farther she got from the dock, and from the ferry—which now represented escape and imprisonment all at the same time, and wasn't that a neat trick?—the more comfortable she felt in her pre-written routine.

"If you look to the left, you'll see our shopping area," she said. "The grocery store is small, but we're expecting weekly supply runs to keep it stocked, and you'll all be able to earn money for extra treats by working around the island. If you choose not to work, that's fine too: the basics have been paid for by our generous patrons. We'll be able to begin some basic farming on the far end of the island in the spring, and that *will* be a requirement for all residents with the physical ability to participate, if only because we'd like to be as independent as possible. The pharmacy is completely free, of course, providing you're picking up basic medications, sanitary supplies, or verified prescriptions—"

On and on she went, until they reached the banked apartments and the small individual homes, all of them fresh and new and still smelling of sawdust and paint, all of them waiting for their first occupants to step inside. She watched as her charges peeled off, one after the other, and then she led the Holland children to the apartment they'd be sharing, tucked between herself and Ami, with two new "aunties" to look after them. This, too, was a part of her job on the island, and while she couldn't say she exactly welcomed it, it was familiar enough that she didn't exactly hate it, either. Somehow, this was what her life had always been moving toward.

Sunset found her standing on the roof of her building with a cold bottle of Coke in her hand, watching as the sun eased its way past the horizon and out of sight. There were footsteps behind her. She didn't turn.

"Nice night," said Mark, stopping a few feet away. "They won't all be."

"Probably not," she agreed. Winter was likely to come to their island with the force of a hammer slamming down. She had nightmares sometimes, about all of them dying when their generators blew in the middle of a cold snap, about all of this being for nothing. They had been gone from their homes and their families and everything for almost three months. The island had come together with incredible, even impossible speed, powered by money and necessity, the two gripping hands that have pulled almost every human achievement up from the mud. It might stand for a hundred years. It might topple in a season.

The only thing that would tell them one way or the other was time. The island had to operate. The doors had to close. The world had to stay outside, and they had to stay inside, and they had to hope, and hope, and hope that they'd be able to keep things that way.

Sometimes hope was all a person really had.

"The kids will settle down. Kids are flexible, and they have a pretty good peer group already coming together," said Mark. "They'll figure themselves out. Hopefully with a minimum of bruises."

"Is it wrong of me to hope that any bullies try to pull something early, so Ami can put them down and make all the other kids understand that we're not going to tolerate that sort of thing?" Sandy twined a lock of hair anxiously around one finger. As one of the only Asian kids at her mostly-white Salt Lake City high school, she had experienced more than her fair share of childhood bullying. The idea of the same thing happening to someone else under her nose was abhorrent.

Wishing for someone like Ami to intervene felt almost like a betrayal of the children, who should have been able to sort things out amongst themselves, but leaving the weaker among them at risk would have been even harder for her to live with. Children would do what they would do. It was up to her, and the rest of the adults, to try to minimize the damage.

"I don't think it's wrong," said Mark. "It's not like she'd hurt them, and kids push until they find the boundaries. Showing them where those boundaries are as early as possible is the sort of thing that probably helps."

"That's good."

"I'm a little more worried about us."

Sandy glanced at him. "Us?"

"Us." Mark gestured between them before sweeping his arm out to indicate the rest of the island. "The adults. We're not going to be the majority of the population for a while, which doesn't matter as much as it would if we were actually trying to be self-sufficient. But I don't know if you've noticed…there aren't that many single people here."

"Oh." Sandy paused. "Oh! Mark, I'm flattered, but—"

"I'm not hitting on you," he said. "You're not my type."

"Too Mormon?" she asked. She'd been the one to reject him first, and yet it was difficult to keep the hurt from her voice. "Because I left the church a long time ago."

"Too female." Mark shrugged. "If I'm lucky, one of the other doctors will bring a hot male nurse with them. It doesn't feel too likely to me. Luck hasn't been with us for a while."

Startled, Sandy laughed. Mark cast a sidelong frown in her direction.

"What?" he asked.

"Did you seriously just say that luck hasn't been with us for a while? Seriously? Look around, Mark." Sandy gestured with both arms, encompassing more of the island than Mark's one. "Morris's disease happened. We work with children—*children*, Mark, nature's little viral incubators—and we didn't get sick. Our boss figured out what was happening before the public panic could start and people could start attacking clinics. She offered us the chance to get out."

"The clinic still burned down," said Mark.

"Which could have been a gas leak."

"It wasn't a gas leak."

Sandy sighed. "I know. But it *could* have been a gas leak."

Mark said nothing.

Dr. Gauley's clinic had been the first, and both of them strongly suspected that she had been responsible for its destruction. There was no way she could have destroyed the others. Pediatric clinics around the country had been burned or bombed or attacked by gun-wielding parents whose grief had blinded them to the reality of what they were doing. Doctors had died. *Children* had died, innocent bystanders in a war that had no clear sides and no clear way of being won. If Dr. Gauley had destroyed her own clinic, she had done it to save lives…and to cover their tracks.

So far as either of them knew, no one outside of their relatively small circle of contractors and candidates knew of the existence of the island. That wasn't going to be the case forever. Things like this had a way of getting out, of being leaked to the wider world. But for now, time was on their side. For now, they could fortify, they could dig in, and they could do it without fear of armed men showing up at their gates, demanding the opportunity to survive.

"We made it to Canada," said Sandy. "We found a benefactor. We found an *island*. It seems to me that either luck or God has been with us every step of the way, and since I don't believe in God anymore, I'm going to have to go with luck. It's that or start questioning every choice I've made since I walked away from Utah—and given how hard Salt Lake was hit by Morris's disease, I don't think that's a good approach to take."

Vaccination rates in Salt Lake City had fallen off in the last few years, with more and more parents taking the approach that vaccines were like alcohol or caffeine, unnecessary poisons for the bodies of their children. As a consequence, the city's herd immunity had been eroded to the point of uselessness. The epidemic had swept through the city, killing no more than the normal percentage of victims, but leaving so many immunocompromised that the city, and the state, would be struggling to fulfill their medical needs for years. Her family, which had previously been willing to cut ties with their strange, unexpectedly atheist daughter, had tried to call her back several times after the outbreak died down, claiming that this was a sign from God that she was needed at home.

If their God communicated by destroying the immune systems of children, she wanted no part of His plan.

"I guess the chips have fallen the way we needed them to fall a few times," admitted Mark.

"A few," Sandy agreed. "Things are going to go wrong soon enough. Things *always* go wrong when you give them long enough. So for right now, how about we enjoy the fact that things are going sort of right? The real work starts tomorrow."

"Yeah." Mark put an arm around her shoulders and kissed her cheek, lightly. "So you know, if I liked girls at all, you'd be at the top of my list. And not only because we're sort of stranded on a private island together."

"Flatterer," said Sandy, and the two of them stood in comfortable silence, and watched the stars come out.

4.

THERE WERE a few private homes on the island, dwellings built away from the more efficient duplexes and apartments. Space was at a premium: every inch needed to be accounted for in order to make the best use of what they had. But the plan had included the possibility of individuals whose mental health required them to have a larger degree of privacy, and had also taken into account the fact that certain individuals with "high value" jobs—jobs like

Dr. Gauley's—might need a degree of isolation if they ever wanted to be allowed to consider themselves off the clock. It was mental health again, taken from a slightly different angle.

Dr. Gauley's home was barely bigger than her San Francisco apartment had been, bedroom and kitchen and postage stamp living room packed into a space that would have been perfectly suited as a mobile home or something else designed to move on a regular basis. In fact, her original proposal for the private residences had been mobile homes, since they would have been moveable if the island's needs changed. Only the logistical difficulty of transporting entire mobile homes, when there was already a construction crew present and ready to assemble any structure they wanted, had convinced her that permanent homes were a better idea.

It was, admittedly, pleasant to have walls thick enough to keep the island noise out. The silence was sometimes deafening this far from the city, and the rest of the time the crash of sea and the roar of the wind were terrifyingly loud, making it impossible to focus on anything else. She walked from the kitchen to the tiny living room, a bottle of wine in one hand and two glasses in the other. Brooke, curled on the couch with her feet tucked up beneath her body, raised her head and smiled.

"You always know exactly the right thing," she said.

"I feel like this is where I should make a joke about being the older sister, but honestly, I'm too frightened of what happens tomorrow to even pretend that I agree with you." Izzy sat, tipping the bottle gently over the glasses. The wine was clear as lymph, and smelled far sweeter. "This is really happening. We're so far beyond the point of taking it back that it's not even worth wondering about. We're going to fill this island with people whose immune systems are intact, and we're going to keep them here until Morris's disease is eradicated. Which may not happen in our lifetimes. You realize that, right? We've just become a private prison for people whose crime was somehow failing to catch the deadliest disease of our generation."

"Sometimes I wonder what my life would be like right now if Lisa hadn't been the first person to die," replied Brooke, and snagged a wine glass. "I don't wonder what it would be like if she'd lived, because I get to see *that* delightful torture every time I go to sleep. I hate dreaming. I hate waking up even more. But fuck, it would have been nice to have this damn disease named after someone other than my dead husband. My dead daughter. The people I loved, who left me because of a fucking *disease*."

Brooke drained her glass in a single convulsive swallow before glaring at Izzy.

"Don't sit there looking guilty," she snapped. "It's not your damn fault you couldn't save them from something no one had ever seen before. If this is anybody's fault, it's mine, for saying 'yes' when she begged to go to that *stupid* theme park. I could have kept her home. I could have kept her healthy. I didn't. If anyone gets to carry guilt around this island like a rock, it's me. Drink your damn wine and don't make that face."

"I'm sorry." Izzy looked away. "It's just that I miss her too."

"She's easy to miss. Sometimes I wonder how we were ever lucky enough to have her in our lives." Brooke raised her empty wineglass in a toast. "To Angela, for being too stupid to understand that she was holding the greatest treasure in the universe."

"To Angela," echoed Izzy. "For being smart enough to understand that she wasn't ready to be a mother, and kind enough to give the rest of us the opportunity to know Lisa."

"Yeah." Brooke reached for the bottle, refilling her glass. "Have you heard from her?"

For one dizzying instant, Izzy thought her sister was talking about Lisa: that she was asking whether the ghost of a dead little girl had followed them as far as the island. The moment, mercifully, passed. Izzy sighed, and held her own glass out for a refill.

"Angela emails me almost every day. She stopped for a little while, when the government was looking into the activities of her little 'political activism' group, but now that she's been cleared of wrongdoing in the destruction of the clinic, she's back to trying to figure out exactly where we are and what we're doing here. She knows she's being left out of something, again, and she wants to understand."

"I wish we could tell her."

"I wish we could too. But Angela never learned a secret she didn't want to share, especially when she thought it could get her the kind of attention she needs." The kind of attention that lit up the world, that made her feel like *she* was the most important sister, and not the one who always seemed to be standing on the outside of the unit formed by Izzy and Brooke, the unit that had slammed shut before Angela could figure out how to get inside.

Izzy had spent her share of time feeling bad about that. She had better things to feel bad about now, and better things to worry about. Angela and her hurt feelings could wait until the world changed into something better.

"We didn't...try." Brooke looked at Izzy uncertainly. "I didn't see any blood test results for her. Did you even check to see whether she'd be able to come with us? Maybe we could have included her. Maybe..."

"We're on an island, despite the logistical problems it creates, despite the fact that we could have purchased three to four times as much land for even less money, because we needed to know that we wouldn't turn around to find people like Angela—like that terrorist group she pretends is political activism—clawing at our gates," said Izzy. "The greatest danger an inland isolation facility would have faced wouldn't have been infection, it would have been people trying to rip down our fences because they wanted what they assumed we had. It's going to be a while before the sheer magnitude of the consequences of Morris's disease becomes clear to the world outside. I want us to use that time to reinforce our walls and lock our doors, not to convince our sister that she can't suddenly become the Patron Saint of Quarantine, or worse, promise every one of her new 'friends' that she has a political hardball for them to play with. I'm sorry. I really am. She's our sister. Despite everything, I do love her. But there was never going to be a place for her here, because we have never lived in a world where she knew how to keep her damn mouth shut."

Brooke laughed bitterly. "Sometimes I wish you were worse at being right."

"I'd also take better at being wrong," said Izzy. She sipped her wine and leaned back in her seat until she was staring at the ceiling. "Sometimes I feel like my whole life has been one long attempt to be the one who gets to be wrong."

"Don't worry." Brooke nudged her sister's leg with her foot. "I'm sure you'll fuck up eventually."

"Count on it," said Izzy, and closed her eyes.

5.

BROOKE WAS snoring gently on the couch, her empty glass dangling from her fingertips. Izzy leaned over and took it away, setting it on the table before drawing an afghan across her sister's shoulders.

"I'm so sorry," she whispered, pressing a kiss against Brooke's forehead. "For everything. I'm so sorry, and I'm going to make it up to you, I promise. Just give me time. That's all I need to show you that we're doing the right thing."

Brooke made a soft snoring sound and nestled deeper under the afghan. Izzy watched her for a moment, as if making sure that she was really asleep, before turning and carrying their glasses to the kitchen.

Rinsing and hanging them only took a few seconds. With that done, she pulled on a pair of latex gloves before she opened the fridge and withdrew a small brown paper package, tied with string. The temperature sticker on the side indicated that it was still quite cold. Even so, she held it well away from herself as she left the house via the back door and made her way down the long central avenue to the ferry dock.

A single boat was still parked there, waiting for the midnight mail to be delivered. Mail leaving the island wasn't subject to nearly as many search protocols, as it was assumed to be clean, no matter what: they were keeping pathogens *out*, not spreading them. Calmly, Izzy dropped her package into the waiting bin. Then she turned, not waiting to be acknowledged, and walked away.

Someday she would get better at being wrong.

Not yet.

"There are always going to be people who insist that vaccination is a personal choice, and that if we take that choice away, we must necessarily take other choices away—that the right to refuse a vaccine is the same as the right to refuse to donate a kidney, or the right to say that no one else is allowed to use your body as a life support system without your full and knowing consent. There are always going to be people willing and ready to use the public health as a political sticking point.

I can see that some of you aren't pleased with this part of my testimony, so allow me to be candid. Morris's disease does not care about your feelings, your opinions, or your attempts to use bodily autonomy as a weapon. Morris's disease *can't* care. All it can do is kill, and it is going to continue to do so, with increasing efficacy, until people stop arguing and start fighting back. We don't have very much time. If we want a chance here, we need to take it, before it's too late."

—from the testimony of Dr. Isabelle Gauley.

PART III: Ashes, Ashes

5: | Infection

1.

THE SECOND major Morris's disease outbreak began in Calgary, Alberta, approximately ten months after the first outbreak had been declared over, and four months after the first major whooping cough outbreak. Despite precautions, it swiftly spread throughout North and South America, and successfully jumped from there to Europe, Asia, and the Pacific Islands. Africa was able to dodge the second outbreak.

It was not so successful with the third.

By the fourth outbreak, the resources of the world were turned almost entirely toward finding a vaccine that could circumvent the lasting damage done by the infection. Following the "wipe" of the immune system by a first exposure, nothing seemed to take, leaving survivors at an increased risk of reinfection by Morris's disease. That, alone, might not have been so terrifying, if not for the equally increased risk of infection by every other viral agent. A world that had been willing to reject the efficacy of vaccines suddenly found itself on the verge of being forced to live without them, and it was not prepared.

In the chaos of the outbreaks and the responses, it was perhaps understandable when no one immediately noticed that a large number of doctors—most of them specialists, none of them so well-known as to be considered leading lights of their fields, but still, solid, competent, valuable professionals—had slipped out of sight, shuttering their practices and leaving their patients scrambling for care. When the disappearance of doctors went unnoticed, it was perhaps equally understandable that no one noticed the disappearance of an even greater number of nurses, technicians, and other individuals.

Had anyone bothered to run facial recognition between the lists of the missing and the hospitals still accepting patients, they might have discovered a surprising number of those individuals moving through crowds far afield of where they had last been seen, dispensing treatments and providing vaccinations. Only to those not yet infected with Morris's disease. Only to those who could still be helped.

Many of the children these individuals vaccinated would later disappear, and their parents—frightened and quiet and determined—would refuse to say where they had gone. One couple stood trial for the murder of their five-year-old, who had vanished following a Morris scare at his school, and whose grandmother had contacted the police. In their case, the jury found them not guilty, but the judge stated, even as she released the couple, that they were clearly hiding *something*.

The feeling that someone was hiding *something* spread, along with the disappearances and the silences from certain parts of the medical profession. It was thus, perhaps, a relief to some when—five years after Lisa Morris woke feeling unwell, almost to the day—a report arrived on the desk of the President of the United States, notifying her that Dr. Isabelle Gauley had been seen on a ferry dock in rural Canada.

The existence of Island One was confirmed three days later, when a group of Canadian customs officers attempting to follow up on the photograph was repelled by a private security force. They returned with additional troops, only to find large QUARANTINE signs hung all the way around the island perimeter, alternating with the PRIVATE PROPERTY signs which had already been present. They retreated to discuss their options, and were met by Mr. Christopher Holland, billionaire, and his army of lawyers.

His ownership of Island One was, it seemed, watertight. Everything had been done legally. The island had been bought outright, and what property taxes he owed to the government had been paid without fail. The permits, the registrations, even the zoning changes necessary for the island's private hospital, they were all in order. There was no reason for outsiders to set foot there—and in fact, due to the regulations Canada had passed following the second outbreak, there were legal reasons to keep them out. All of them, even the military. As there had been no complaints from the individuals on the island, and Dr. Gauley was not wanted by the United States for any reason more complex than curiosity, there was no reason for the quarantine to be broken.

When it was asked—as it inevitably must be—what could possibly be on the island that was so terrible it warranted a complete lockdown, Mr. Holland replied with a bitter laugh, and the statement, "We're not protecting you from the island. We're protecting the island from you."

Every major news outlet in North America carried the story within twenty-four hours. Secret enclaves, free of Morris's disease, hidden under the noses of the public. The temerity! The indignity!

The outrage. People began swarming for Island One, expecting to be allowed to force, beg, or bribe their way inside, and were stunned to be met with calm, armed resistance. Ami had trained her team well, and had done it over the course of years. Every one of them knew how much they had to lose, both collectively and individually. Every one of them had a family member, or a close friend, or a child with them on the island, waiting out the medical miracles that would be necessary to make it possible for them to walk free. Every one of them was willing to die, if that was what it came to, in order to keep those people safe.

They were isolated. Travel to the island was never going to be easy, no matter how much money someone had, no matter how desperate they were. The further waves of angry citizens demanding entry never materialized.

Six months later, a hacker who had managed to latch onto the email traffic coming out of Island One was able to pinpoint the location of Island Two, off the coast of Maine. This facility was harder to protect, thanks to the United States government being willing to be persuaded with bribes to send the Coast Guard to "investigate." Both islands had been expecting that; the truly vulnerable had been evacuated to other facilities months earlier. Everyone who was present when the Coast Guard broke through the quarantine line had volunteered to stay.

Of the two hundred and seventy-four people on Island Two, all of whom had been certified clean of Morris's disease, eighteen showed symptoms immediately after exposure to the newcomers.

Six died. The other twelve were removed from the island system, no longer able to meet the terms of their employment.

(If anyone found it strange that so few people became ill when they had supposedly been isolated since the first outbreak, the shock of the six deaths was sufficient to silence the strangeness. No one searched the private office of Island Two's primary physician. No one discovered the vaccine. The twelve who had allowed themselves to be infected for the sake of the system were compensated well, and not required to seek new employment. Things continued, as things so often do.)

The violation of Island Two resulted in a swift, firm response from Holland, Inc., the parent corporation for the entire island structure. They brought multiple lawsuits against everyone involved in breaching the quarantine line, and paid the legal bills for the twelve survivors and the families of the six dead as they did the same. When people objected, saying that a virus was not a hostile action, that no one could sue someone because they happened to breathe while infected, the corporation's lawyers—who were very, very good, and had been paid very, very well—countered with pictures of the quarantine signs, and the calm reminder that these people had done everything in their power to remove themselves from the risk. They had chosen voluntary exile over the possibility of the very deaths they had been forced to face.

The damages ordered by the jury were exorbitant.

The entire island structure was revealed to the world a week after the end of the trial.

Thirty islands around the world, some "island" in name only—isolated patches of inland territory that were isolated and protected, in one way or another, by geography and distance.

Thirty places with fences and signs and precautions against Morris's disease, thirty places where people were working, not toward a vaccine or a treatment or any of the other things that fell under the purview of a dozen governmental agencies, a hundred governments, but toward the survival of the human race.

"Nearly half our residents are immunocompromised in some way that has nothing to do with Morris's disease," said Dr. Isabelle Gauley via a video interview, during which she deftly deflected questions about whose idea the islands had been. "We have cancer survivors, people who have had organ transplants, people whose immune systems are simply unable to build sufficient resistance to disease. By surrounding them with as many healthy people as we can, as many people untouched by the recent outbreaks, we're able to protect them until greater minds than ours can come up with a solution."

When asked whether the islands were open to additional residents, her face fell, and she shook her head. "We continued to recruit as long as we could; we wanted a diverse population with the skills for self-sufficiency. We have no room at this time, and even if we did, the requirements, health-wise, are simply unrealistic for someone who has been in the general population for the last five years. The chances of anyone being able to survive that many outbreaks of Morris's disease without even a low-grade infection are too low. We can't afford to risk our technicians in screening people who will never be able to make it past the quarantine."

Ami and the other security chiefs doubled, and then tripled, the patrols around all island properties.

Island Twenty-One, located in a previously untouched stretch of Calgary forest, was stormed by panicked parents looking for a way to save their children, and burned to the ground with more than half the residents, some under the age of eighteen, still inside. The survivors were immediately collected by Holland Inc. copters and SUVs, but several were still infected, including three-year-old Danielle Vargas, who had been born in the facility, and whose parents had both been killed in the fire. She died shortly after. There was no one left to make decisions about her burial. Following her cremation, Christopher Holland himself took her ashes home, placing them on the mantel alongside members of his own family.

"This ends here," he said.

The world, mercifully, listened.

Even more mercifully, when a parent in Illinois came forward a year later to claim that her missing daughter was present in the background of an illegal satellite photo of Island One, no one listened. The raids did not resume.

The quarantine held.

All the rest came after.

2.

"AUNT IZZY?"

Dr. Isabelle Gauley—older now, slower now, shoulders bent by ten years as the only pediatrician of a small island community whose children could never, no matter how much they wanted to, leave—turned away from her desk and smiled at the little girl in the doorway.

"Hello, Michelle," she said. "What can I do for you today?"

Michelle beamed. She wasn't really Izzy's niece. Only David was *really* related to Aunt Izzy, and he was her nephew, not her niece. Which meant Michelle was double extra special, because her mommy was Aunt Izzy's best friend and that meant she got to be a niece anyway, even if she wasn't really.

"Mommy said to come and tell you that she's going to the dock to meet the mail, and if you have any packages she can bring them back, and also she's leaving me here in your office while she makes the walk." Michelle smiled winsomely.

Izzy swallowed the urge to laugh. If Sandy was dropping Michelle off for unplanned babysitting, that meant Ivan had suddenly found himself with a hole in his schedule, and she wanted to try for a third child. She was allowed—despite the lack of space on the island, birth rates were not as yet restricted, and even if they had been, Isabelle's position was that replacement was always allowed. Isabelle wasn't planning to have children. If Sandy, or Brooke, or even Mark wanted to use her "slot," they were more than welcome.

"Did she tell you why she wasn't asking me first?" she asked.

Michelle nodded vigorously. "She wanted it to be a *surprise*."

"Well, then, your mother was very successful, and success should be rewarded. But since she's not here, I guess we'll have to eat our reward ourselves, won't we?"

"Reward?" Michelle's eyes widened, even as her voice dropped to a conspiratorial whisper. "Do you mean…cookies?"

"I *do*. I *do* mean cookies." Izzy slid out of her seat and started toward the cupboard at the other side of the room, the six-year-old immediately and firmly at her side.

Junk food was allowed on Island One—something that wasn't the case at all facilities. Island Six was vegan; Island Eight enforced a strict "foods we can grow for ourselves" diet. But Island One had been the first, and the rules hadn't been quite so clear-cut when they were getting started, and by the time it had occurred to her, or Brooke, or anyone that they could potentially limit the items allowed past the dock, it had been too late. Chocolate and chips and all the little pleasures of home were an established part of the island's culture.

Privately, Izzy was glad. The children like Michelle, who were born and raised here, could take the little things they missed out on as ordinary: they had never begged to go to a theme park, for example, because they didn't know what a theme park *was*. Outside pen pals weren't allowed until age thirteen, and even then, more internet access would be afforded if they chose a pen pal from another island facility. Yes, the internet was censored, and yes, access to the outside world was restricted, and no, she was not sorry. She would never *be* sorry. These were her people. It was her job to keep them safe until the rest of the world managed to get its act together.

Michelle was babbling happily about her class and the things they were learning, how important they were, how fun they were to know. Izzy made the appropriate sounds of agreement and inquiry, gauging which was appropriate by the tone of the girl's voice, and let the words wash over her virtually unheard. She didn't need the specifics. Life here was calm, linear, predictable, and that was how she liked it. A simple life.

Outside, outbreaks of Morris's disease still happened periodically, casting the world into chaos. A working vaccine existed, for the people who had yet to be infected, but there were debates about how to treat those whose immune systems had already been damaged. As they were the majority, it was difficult to proceed. Children grew up in virtual isolation. Izzy strongly doubted that any of them were demanding trips to amusement parks, either.

Here, there was freedom, within an admittedly limited scope. Here, there was room to run beneath a big blue sky, and a small, loving, passionate community of people weathering out the storm in relative health and safety. It wasn't perfect—it could never have been perfect—and so many people were dead that sometimes it boggled the mind when she tried to think about it, but it was good. It was good, and it was going to keep on getting better.

The islands had everything they needed to keep going for another twenty years. That would be enough. Twenty years would mean the world got a grip on how it approached public health, how it handled issues like vaccination and quarantine and everything else. Twenty years would *fix* things. The immunosuppressant effects of Morris's disease might even prove to be a blessing in disguise, in some ways: they had forced medicine to come to terms with the fact that immunity wasn't a choice some people didn't make, but was instead a function of being alive in the world. More care was being taken. In so many areas, more care was being taken.

The world that was going to rise out of the ashes of Morris's disease would be better, and cleaner, and kinder. People would be more understanding of the fact that their choices had an impact on others. It was going to *work*. And the islands were going to produce the next generation of leaders for that world, people who had grown up safe and protected, by adults who had given up virtually everything to make sure they would have the best possible chances, the best possible choices.

Michelle had stopped talking and was looking at her expectantly. Izzy smiled and opened the cupboard with a flourish.

"Cookies!" she announced.

Michelle cheered.

They were sitting at Izzy's desk, dipping chocolate chip cookies in milk and giggling, their heads pressed close together, when the office door opened half an hour later. Both of them looked up. Izzy smiled. Michelle beamed.

"Aunt Izzy gave me cookies!" she announced.

"Good for you, boo," said Sandy. Time had been kind to her. There were a few streaks of gray in her hair, and the pink barrettes she used to keep it out of her face looked less like a fashion choice and more like something she had stolen from her daughter's dresser, but she was still recognizably herself, still pleasant and open and unchanged by a decade surrounded by the sea. A plain gold band reflected the light from her left hand, a reminder of her wedding, held on the easternmost beach, while the sun was setting and Ivan held her hands, looking like he thought he was the luckiest man on Earth.

In so many ways, he was. Morris's disease hadn't taken anyone from his immediate family, hadn't infected his body, and had brought him to the island where his true love was waiting. All it had been, for Ivan, was the virus that changed the world.

"Sorry to drop her on you like that," said Sandy, shifting her attention to Izzy. Her cheeks colored faintly. "There wasn't any mail for you."

"Somehow I didn't expect there would be," Izzy mildly replied. "Did you have a nice time?"

"Yes," said Sandy, voice a little too prim to be believable. "Did you?"

"Honestly? Yes, we did." Izzy's glance at Michelle was nothing but fond. "It was nice to have an excuse to eat cookies and not worry for a while."

"Worry?" Sandy's brow furrowed. "About what?"

"Only the usual. There's nothing to concern yourself about, and I promise you I'll tell you if that changes." Izzy made a shooing gesture with her hands. "But as the site administrator, this is where I tell you I need to go back to work if I want to go home tonight. So I love you both dearly, but get out."

"Bye, Aunt Izzy," said Michelle, and leaned over to give the older woman a kiss on the cheek before grabbing her remaining cookies and darting to her mother's side, clutching them like the greatest treasure in the world. Which, to her, they were.

"Bye, bug," said Izzy. She sipped her crumb-studded milk as she watched the pair exit, and waited until the external door closed before allowing her shoulders to relax and turning back to her computer.

Research teams in Atlanta and Toronto were close to cracking the protein structure that made Morris's disease such an efficient killer. Once they'd done that, they'd be able to find a cure. She'd honestly expected them to succeed years ago; she'd believed the death tolls and the after-effects would have been enough to cut through the political bullshit and posturing and make people understand that ideological differences had no place in this particular debate. Remove the threats to bodily autonomy and treat vaccination as a matter of public good. Accept that saying "we will not mandate vaccination because God may disapprove" was the same as saying "we are willing to let our most vulnerable die," and either change or own the monstrosity of it all.

She had believed, one last time, in the better natures of humanity, and she had been disappointed, as always. But now, they were finally on the right track. More and more, vaccination was being treated as a necessity for having a global community. More and more, the response to fearmongering and unnecessary political posturing was a firm refusal to engage. The world was in danger. People needed to be saved.

This had all lasted so much longer than it needed to.

Her email was, as always, a series of complicated moral issues, some of them presented openly, some presented in careful code. She answered what she could, deleted what didn't apply to her, and sent the message, over and over again, for people to hold the ground they had, to wait and see. Maybe this new treatment would work. Maybe these new researchers would break the protein shell and find the way to turn people's immune systems back on, rendering the world safer than it had ever been. That same research would enable them, eventually, to help those who had become immunocompromised via non-Morris means. She was sure of it.

Izzy closed her laptop and rose, stretching until she felt her back pop. They'd been on the island longer than she had ever expected, but that wasn't such a bad thing. It had been good to her. It had been good to all of them.

The sidewalks—not streets; there were no real streets here— were as busy as they ever were, residents making their way between home and shops and amusements. Most people waved at her, some calling her name. She waved gladly back. They had their problems, their little conflicts and troubles, but they were happy. They knew the size and shape of their world, and they liked it.

Once the doors were finally open, she had faith that some of the island children would choose to come back and make their lives here. The community would last, even as the world began repairing itself. There were worse things.

The school—the Lisa Morris Memorial Schoolhouse— was shuttered for the day. She cut through the playground and descended the small rise to her house. The door, as always, was unlocked. Only the medical offices ever bothered locking their doors, and that for the sake of safety.

She let herself inside. She turned on the light.

Angela, sitting in the chair across from the front door, raised her head and smiled thinly.

"Hello, Isabelle," she said.

3.

THE WORLD froze. The world shattered. The world snapped back into focus, becoming a real, full-color thing once again. Izzy stared, her heart thrashing in her chest, before slowly turning and closing the door. She flipped the long-disused deadbolt with her thumb as she took her hand away.

"How did you get here?" she asked softly. Ami would be furious. Her security systems were supposed to be unbreakable.

"It took some time," said Angela. "I had to find a ferry driver who was willing to be bribed, and I couldn't do that directly without tipping you off. How many of them have family here? Clever way of guaranteeing loyalty you don't deserve."

Izzy said nothing.

"Once I made it to the island, I went diving. The water's cold, but there's equipment for that. You should really check the sensitivity of your motion detectors on the west shore."

Of course. The seals used the west shore as a breeding ground; they couldn't keep the motion detectors turned all the way up, or they'd be sending resources to that point constantly. It was a known weakness. They'd all assumed that the remoteness, the loyalty of the ferry drivers, the temperature of the water, would protect them. If anything was going to be the downfall of mankind, it wouldn't be the tribalism, the prejudice, the wars. It would be the *assumptions*.

"What are you doing here?" asked Izzy. "It isn't safe."

"Your precious herd immunity can handle one filthy outsider." Angela leaned forward, suddenly smiling. "I want to know how much you're going to offer me, and I want to see your face while I ask for it."

"What do you mean?"

"I mean that everyone here thinks of you as Dr. Gauley the savior, Dr. Gauley the genius who found a way to save a little slice of the world from chaos. Dr. Gauley the pediatrician. The healer of children." Angela's lip curled. "It's honestly amazing to me that no one bothered to dig into your background enough to find your ex-husband."

For the second time in a handful of minutes, Izzy said nothing.

"He's dead, by the way. Morris's disease. I'm sure you're so very *sorry* to hear that one of the only people who remembered Dr. Isabelle Charles is gone. He could have told the world so many interesting things about your post-graduate research, back when you were going to be a virologist. Back when you were going to save the world from death and disease. Back before that anti-vaccination group caused the last Zika outbreak."

Silence.

"Did you even get the chance to name your baby?"

Silence.

"It was so surprising when you decided to go into pediatrics, like you wanted to surround yourself with what you'd never have. But you seemed so happy, and our parents supported you, and you and Brooke were working together, and when she couldn't have a child you somehow managed to convince me she should end up with mine, and now my daughter's dead and you're still the golden child, you're still perfect. Still saving the world." Angela smiled. "You're always saving the world."

"You should leave here. Now."

"You deleted almost everything, but you forgot about Matthew's private cloud server."

Izzy stared.

"I think the world is going to be *very* interested in the blueprint for Morris's disease, don't you? They'll probably be able to cure it faster. They'll definitely be able to trace it back to its creator. Maybe Brooke will finally like me best. That would be nice. We can mourn my daughter together."

Izzy's voice was small and steady. "You won't do that."

"Watch me." Angela stood. "You did this. You have so much blood on your hands. It's time the world knew."

Izzy sighed and stepped away from the locked door. "Was this your whole plan? To come here and tell me I'm a monster, like you thought I didn't know? Like you thought I hadn't already done the math and decided I would rather be a monster than a martyr? Did you at least bring a gun?"

Angela hesitated. "I didn't...what?"

"No. Of course not," said Izzy, and reached below the mail table, pulling loose the pistol she kept hidden there.

The gunshot was very loud. Angela didn't have time to blink before she fell, a hole at the center of her forehead.

"That's the thing about monsters, Angie," said Izzy, lowering the gun. "It takes one to know one."

4.

ANGELA GAULEY'S body was never found. The currents off the western edge of the island were too strong for that, and the local marine life too hungry. Work on a cure for the aftereffects of Morris's disease continued; the name "Dr. Isabelle Charles" went unspoken.

The quarantine held. The islands thrived.

All the rest came after.